MW01204403

# Shall Be

Written by Laveau White

Cover Design by Laveau White

Edited by Laveau White

www.authorlaveau.com

This story is completely fictional. Some places may be real but the events surrounding them are not. Any names or situations that may be similar to actual events is completely coincidental.

The version of the Bible used in this book is the King James Version.

## Acknowledgements

*I would first like to thank my Lord and Savior Jesus Christ for allowing me to operate in the gifts he has given me. I also thank God for the supportive family that he has blessed me with.*

*To my husband Keith and my children Kyla and Jaxon, I would like to thank you for supporting me through anything I want to accomplish. Keith you believed in me before I had this gift to offer. I love you.*

*Mom and Dad, Lavoe and Duane Jackson, thank you for forever having my back no matter what. You have been my supporters in life, and I love and appreciate you both.*

*To all my sisters, Bianca, Gabrielle, and Viva I love you all. Whether sisters by blood or life, you are the sisters that I have been blessed to share my life and experiences with and I am forever grateful to the Creator.*

*Special mentions to Fior Baptiste (My Ronnie), Gabrielle (My Gabby), Keith (My Hubby), Cynthia (My #1 Fan, and Viva (My Sister/Friend) for being a very present help and influence during the writing of this book. As always, thank you all for your support!*

# Dedications

I would like to dedicate this book to my children and the reason for my self-reflection, Kyla, Jaxon, Lindsey, and Jacob.

Kyla, you have shown me that although some lessons are learned the hard way, they are learned none the less, with wisdom beyond their years. Keep on shining and remember that everything is possible for you!

Jaxon, my baby boy, you have shown me that is is very possible to learn from the mistakes of others (Kyla). Continue to do what you know to be right; listen to the God inside of you!

Lindsey, my bonus baby, your determination to do the things you set out to do is inspiring. Thank you for allowing me into your life. I am so proud of you!

Jacob, no amount of time or distance can change the love I have for my first-born son. In these past two years, I have seen you grow and mature into a man that I am proud to know. Thank you for finding me!

# Chapter One

## "Get out!"

She can tell that the room is spinning before lifting her eyelids. Kyla slowly opens her eyes as she sits upright on the couch, hoping that her equilibrium quickly stabilizes before her stomach reacts to the vertigo. Still completely dressed from the night before, she stumbles to the bathroom, holding on to every wall along the way. After turning on the shower, she looks in the mirror and takes inventory of her face as she does every morning. The bags under red eyes, the imprint from her leather couch on the left side of her face, the barely noticeable scar on her forehead that she got in a fight at age sixteen, her caramel skin, her mother's round chestnut eyes, and her father's round nose, all reminders of the last thirty-six years of her life. As she pulls her shoulder length hair into a bun, she can hear keys rattling at the front door before it opens and closes.

"Babe?! Sorry it took me so long to get home! I had to work out some money issues with Jerome! You know every time we promote a party that chump tries to get over! Babe?!"

Arron makes his way through the condo and finally finds Kyla standing at the bathroom sink, looking in the mirror.

"Babe, did you hear me?"

Kyla's expressionless eyes shift to Arron's reflection in the mirror. She takes in all six-foot-two of his muscular, milk chocolate frame, remembering a time when she was very much in love with him.

"Yeah, I always hear you."

She turns slowly to look him directly in his hazel eyes.

"I hear you every time you come in, mid-morning, smelling like somebody's bitch, high, and lying to me. But this time you can't lie. You think I didn't see you take that whore in the back of the club?" She says, in a dangerously even tone.

"W-what are you talking about Ky? You were three sheets to the wind last night. You can't trust drunk judgement." Arron dismissively spews before walking away.

Kyla follows swiftly behind him into the bedroom.

"The only thing that's wrong with *my* judgement is the fact that you're still here. I wasn't so drunk that I couldn't get up and follow you and your slut to a back corner of the club, where you casually commence to please her orally and have unprotected sex with her."

Kyla stands in the doorway with her arms crossed, staring at the back of Arron's head as he sits stiffly on the bed. After a few silent moments, he chuckles under his breath and slowly shakes his head.

"Why do we even go through this shit, man?" His tone is completely dispassionate. "You get mad and talk a bunch of nonsense, but when it comes down to it, I'm still here. I mean, by now you know what it is, right? So, go get in the shower and get over it . . . like you always do."

He never once turns to look at her, and Kyla's once calm demeanor has now turned to climaxing rage.

"Get over it?! How about you get the hell out! Like now, not later!" she screams.

"Are you really about to do this?" Arron lets out a sigh of frustration and finally turns to face Kyla. "I need to get some sleep."

"Get out!" she says.

Kyla begins to take Arron's clothing from the dresser drawers. Arron jumps up from the bed.

"What are you doing?"

"Get out!" Kyla says again while moving to the closet to remove more of Arron's belongings.

"Stop pulling my shit out!" he yells.

The tone of his voice causes Kyla to stop in her tracks. Without a word, she leaves the room, but Arron continues in his rant as he returns his clothes to their "rightful" place.

"Bitch think she is?" he mumbles. "Hell you gone put me outta MY house! I should make yo' crazy ass get ou. . ."

The sound of a high-powered stun gun cuts his statement short. PTZZZ! Arron turns to see Kyla standing in the doorway with her stun gun in one hand and a baseball bat in the other. She takes a deep breath and then speaks in the most frighteningly calm voice Arron has ever heard from her lips. He didn't know if he should forget his clothes and leave now, or if it is safer to take his belongings with him.

"Take those clothes out of MY drawers and out of MY closet, and get out of MY house, right now. You have disrespected me for the past five years and now it's enough. And I'll be the first to admit that it's all my fault. But now, I'm doing what I should have done the day I met you. . . walk the hell away."

He can see the disgust and bitter disinterest in her eyes. So, he counts this as a loss and packs his own clothing as she stands in the doorway swinging the Louisville slugger. Arron has never seen her respond with such finality. Usually, he can see a light at the end of the tunnel, a glimmer in her eye that tells him to say the right thing so that she can forgive him. But, not today. She has no more time or energy for him.

Arron carries a suitcase and drags two garbage bags to his Camaro. He makes his final trip into the condo to grab a box filled with toiletries. As he retrieves the box, he searches Kyla's eyes for some sign of affection, but he finds nothing.

In a last-ditch effort to polish his terribly tarnished reputation, Arron asks one last question as he steps outside the door, "You do know I love you, right?"

Kyla slams the door in his face before he can form another word. Defeated, Arron slowly makes his way to his car. He sits for a moment, hoping his emotional companion will come to her senses. After waiting ten minutes or so, he finally decides that the best thing to do is to leave.

Meanwhile, Kyla lights a cigarette and pours a shot of tequila. She doesn't care that she's still hungover from the night before. She sits on the cream leather sofa that she had been all but glued to not even a half-hour before. The shower, now running cold water, can be heard in the distance, almost as if to drown out the last five years of her life. He heart is broken, but she can't seem to conjure the emotion to shed tear.

Now at the end of her cigarette, she takes the shot of tequila and slams the glass on the contemporary marble coffee table.

"Good riddance!"

# Chapter Two

## "I'm getting too old for this."

Being CFO of a profitable finance company is a bonus when you're hungover and heart broken. Kyla enters the seventeenth floor of the One Metropolitan Square building wearing the darkest shades she can find. She wears all black as if to mourn the passing of her deceased relationship.

"Good morning, Ms. LaRue!" Jenna, Kyla's secretary squeals in her normal annoyingly chipper style. "You have messages from . . ."

"Email them to me please."

Jenna is cut off before she can finish her sentence.

"Please get me a cup of coffee." Kyla continues. "Oh and hold all my calls." She spews, as she walks into her office without missing a step in her stride along the way.

She closes the door behind her and leaves the light off. Once the shades are closed and lowered, Kyla feels it's safe to remove her glasses. The pain in her head is excruciating and the 1,600 milligrams of Ibuprofen has not done the trick. It has barely numbed the pain in her abdomen.

"I'm getting too old for this." she whispers into her computer keyboard as she holds her head in both hands.

Finally, her fingers, seemingly on autopilot, type the username and password to her computer. She opens her email, and as requested Jenna has emailed her messages.

"Where's my coffee?" Kyla mumbles.

The first message is from Jameca, Kyla's friend since high school, requesting a call back as soon as possible. When she sees Arron's name in the subject line of the second message Kyla deletes the email immediately.

She rolls around to the large window and slowly opens the blinds. Looking out of the window to admire the Arch through the buildings that threaten to compare themselves to the height of her office window, she contemplates calling Jameca. She takes a deep breath before turning to pick up the phone and prepares herself for a conversation with her needy best-friend.

Jameca Wilborn, is half Puerto Rican, half Haitian, and is a successful neurosurgeon. They've been friends since middle-school. But, just like every other relationship in her life, things began to change. She realizes that Jameca seems to draw closer when Kyla is the least happy. Not for the purpose of comfort like a true friend, but to gloat about how well her life is going and how happy she is about her own circumstances. As if to jolt herself back into reality, Kyla swiftly rolls back around to enormous red oak desk, picks up the phone, and dials her friend's phone number. After a few rings, Jameca obnoxiously answers.

"Jenna, tell that bitch to stop treating me like a client!"

"Jameca, it's me." Kyla says with no enthusiasm. "Is that really how you talk to my secretary?"

"Look, I need to meet for lunch. I have something very important to ask you. But it's got to be in person." Jameca says, completely ignoring Kyla's question.

"When and where?"

While barely listening to Jameca, Kyla notices another email from Jenna with the subject line reading, "Urgent message from Dr. Okai".

"Um, hello?" Jameca interrupts. "I said, La Mancha at 12:30."

Kyla, now preoccupied with her new message, casually agrees to meet and hangs up without saying goodbye. She stares at the unopened email before reluctantly opening the message.

Message: It is urgent that you return a call to Dr. Okai's office as soon as possible. 314-555-6724.

15

She went to her doctor last week because she had not been feeling quite herself. But Kyla is not in the mood to hear her doctor's speech about cigarettes and alcohol. As she ponders whether or to call Dr. Okai now or later, she receives a call from Arron. Since her ringer has been off since his eviction from her condo, she had been able to easily ignore him. The last thing she wants to hear is Arron's voice, but she can't resist the yearning to hear him distraught and begging. So, she waits for him to leave a voicemail.

*"Kyla, I just want to say I'm sorry for everything I said. You didn't deserve that. I really been thinking, and I know I've made a lot of mistakes. The gambling, the cheating, and even the pills. Look, I'll do whatever it takes to come back home. Yeah, I said home. That's right baby, you are home to me. And that's why you can't leave me like this. I need you. Please answer the phone or call me back. We really need to talk."*

Kyla laughs and deletes the message. She looks at her phone and shakes her head with a smirk of utter disbelief.

"Negro, it's only been three hours."

# Chapter Three

## "Man, I need some new friends."

When Kyla arrives at La Mancha Coffee House, Jameca is already sitting at a table in the corner, nursing a hot cup of Ethiopian coffee. As Kyla approaches, she takes note of Jameca's flawless milk chocolate skin and her long, black, silky head of hair. She admires her beauty but is well aware that she possesses a very ugly side when she is not satisfied with the people or things around her. Even Kyla wonders why they've remained friends for so long but realizes that they may be more alike that she is willing to admit.

"Hey." Kyla says dryly as she approaches the table to sit.

"Um, hey! There's no sun in here." Jameca looks around the restaurant as if to seek out the imaginary sun.

"These lights may as well be the sun right now."

"Hungover, huh?" Jameca recognizes the obvious.

"That's an understatement. I need some coffee." Kyla rubs her temples.

"Excuse me! Can you please bring my friend some coffee!" Jameca yells, causing Kyla even more agony.

"Thanks." Kyla says sarcastically.

Per her request, the waiter brings Kyla's coffee and Jameca's previously ordered turkey sandwich on sourdough bread.

"So, what's so important that it couldn't' wait until later or be discussed over the phone?" Kyla carefully removes her glasses and squints until her eyes adjust.

"No, you first. What the hell is going on with you?" Jameca looks Kyla up and down before sipping her coffee.

"I broke up with Arron."

"Again?"

"No, for real this time. I made him pack his garbage and get out." Kyla says determinately.

"So, what happened this time?"

She looks at Jameca with eyes of shame. She has told her so many times of the "Tales of Arron", as if it were a weekly television drama. So, she feels that Jameca is desensitized where Arron is concerned. Kyla prepares herself for the "I told you so's" and blurts out the horrific scene at the club.

"I watched him have sex with a stranger in the back of Jerome's club. I didn't say anything, I just watched while he did things to a woman he just met, that I thought was only for me; only for us." She is actually disgusted and saddened by the thought. "It was like a car wreck." She pauses momentarily at the memory of the last time she felt this way. "I didn't want to watch, but I couldn't turn away! But I think it was what I needed to let him go." Kyla twirls a promise ring around her finger while she talks.

She is so used to wearing the ring Arron gave her three years ago that she hadn't even realized she is still wearing it. She ponders whether or not she is ready to take it off the finger she once thought would wear a permanent symbol of his affection.

"So, does this mean that we're really done with that loser?"

"Yeah, Meke, I'm done."

"Good! When's the last time you saw Caleb? And how's your dad?" Jameca speaks as if to get Kyla out of the way so she won't be interrupted when she finally decides to discuss business concerning herself.

"Caleb actually relapsed again. And with my dad's condition after the fall, I didn't even want to mention my brother to him."

"Oh my God! Your dad fell? When? Why didn't you tell me?" Jameca seems almost too concerned.

"It was a few days ago, and I didn't know you cared so much." Kyla facetiously sneers. "Physically, he's fine. But his mental health is failing. He keeps talking about my mother like she's still alive. Can you take a look at him for me?"

"Of course, anything for Theo. You know I've always had a crush on your dad." She smiles.

"That's not funny!" Kyla is not at all amused and even seems almost angry.

"Just kidding! Geesh." Jameca says, noticing the tension. "Any who! How long had Caleb been clean?"

"About six months. And the last time my dad saw him he was doing pretty good. I don't want to break his heart with this. He was so proud that Caleb was finally getting it together." She shakes her head in disappointment. "But I'm sure you didn't come here to hear about my tragic life."

"Friend, I want to hear whatever you need to say."

It's times like these when Jameca shows actual traits of a true friend.

"Thank you. But I need some good news and I know you have some or else there would be no need for all the suspense. Spit it out!"

Jameca inhales deeply and then smacks her left hand flat on the table to expose a two-karat diamond.

"Girl, Jeff asked me to marry him!" She squeals.

As happy as Kyla is for her friend, she can't help but to see her own failures in Jameca's happiness. Somehow, Jameca has managed to make her feel worse about her life, again. But Kyla begins to wonder how she can blame Jameca for being happy and making choices that make her happy.

"That's wonderful, Meke! I'm so happy for you guys! Have you set a date?"

"Yes, August 1st! And Ky. . . I want you to be my Maiden of Honor!"

Kyla is honored and mortified at the same time. She despises wedding parties. But how does she say no to her closest friend during one of the most momentous times of her life?

"Of course, I will."

The women lean in to embrace one another. And then comes the straw that breaks the camel's back.

"You know, I always thought you'd be my Matron of Honor. But you're beautiful, intelligent, and successful. We'll find the right one for you yet."

BOOM. Lifted up to be dropped again. Kyla looks at Jameca and watches as her lips move, but her thoughts won't allow her to absorb a word. All she can think is. . .

"Man, I need some new friends."

# Chapter Four

## "This is a new low!"

Lunch is finally over, and Kyla has no intentions of going back to the office. In fact, the mention of her father makes her feel obligated to visit him. She checks her phone to see the sixth missed call from Arron. The headache has subsided, but now the pitch-black sunglasses make her feel less visible to strangers that she feels are attempting to read her through her eyes.

Beauty and success are no match for insecurity induced by years of secrets and lies. The past has been a catalyst to her distrust and low expectations of the men in her life. As she pulls into the parking lot, Kyla suppresses her feelings and recalls the unmatched love and respect she has for her ailing father, Theo. It was only three years ago when her mother died of emphysema. And although divorced for two years at that point, Theo's health has deteriorated rapidly and seemingly for no reason at all, since her mother's death.

Now in the rehabilitation ward of Veteran's Hospital, Theo spends most of his time thumbing through old pictures of his family, before his and Shilynne's divorce. When Kyla enters his room, Theo is looking at a picture that appears thirty years old or more. Kyla quietly approaches her father as she watches him smiling in admiration of a time when he was happiest.

"Hi Daddy! What you got there?"

Theo, slightly startled, momentarily takes his attention away from the picture.

"That's my wife." He says, turning back to look at the photo.

"I know Daddy. You and Momma looked really good on that picture. She was so beautiful." Kyla says, now also admiring the picture.

Her mother was a beautiful, petite, light-skinned, bombshell. And her dad was the most handsome, strong, dark-skinned man she had ever known.

"My son came to see me! He's such a good boy."

"Caleb was here? When?" There is concern in her tone.

"Um, it was today. No, it was yesterday, I think." Theo seems confused.

Kyla immediately begins to check for missing valuables.

"What did he want?" She asks, as she frantically searches the room.

"What? He's my son. He just came to see me!" Then he whispers, "Oh, and he checked my safe to make sure these people aren't stealing from me."

She hurriedly grabs his keys to check the safe. Just as she suspects, Caleb has taken every dime of the money that was in it. Thank goodness Kyla made the decision to become a signer on her dad's bank account before his mind began to go and keeps most of his money in his account.

"Damn it!" Kyla spews before she realizes it.

"Excuse me, is something wrong?"

Not wanting to alarm him, Kyla decides she will replace the money and confront Caleb herself.

"No, everything is fine."

"Can you do me a favor?" Theo asks her sincerely.

"Anything for you."

"Call my daughter Kyla for me."


After unsuccessfully trying to get her father to recognize her, Kyla heads directly to where she knows she will find Caleb; the dope house. She pulls up to a building that appears to be vacant except for the unsavory characters sitting on the porch. She discretely removes her jewelry before exiting and locking her vehicle.

"Is Caleb in there?" Kyla asks an obvious addict sitting on the porch, barely coherent.

"Yeah." He hardly got out before nodding into unconsciousness.

Familiar with the process, Kyla lets herself into the house and makes her way to the room where she has found her brother in the past. She walks through the cold, dank, and dark hallway, filled with the stench of urine and chemicals. Finally, she makes it to the room with seven junkies, including Caleb, indulging in their drug of choice. While an eighth earns her right for another hit, by performing fellatio on a dope boy in the corner of the room. Adapting to the element around her, Kyla pretends to see nothing as she approaches Caleb, nodding in and out of coherency in the opposite corner.

"Caleb." Kyla whispers loudly, as she attempts to slap her brother into consciousness. "Caleb!" She's louder this time, when she gives him a slap that jolts him awake, but only for a moment.

"Huh? Wha'? Kyla? Whatchu doin' here?" He's has difficulty pronouncing his words.

29

"Where's Daddy's money?!" Kyla's voice is forceful and angry as she shakes his shoulders to keep him awake long enough to get some answers.

"Wha' mo-ney?"

Kyla began frantically searching his pockets for any remaining money. But all she finds is a small folded piece of paper containing the remainder of Caleb's heroine and obviously the last of Theo's stolen money.

"Stealing from Daddy Caleb? This is a new low!" Kyla is utterly disgusted with him. "You're not allowed to go back to the hospital. Stay away from Daddy and stay away from me!" Kyla's final words before leaving Caleb to waddle in his destructive addiction.

# Chapter Five

## "What in the world did I do?"

The past twenty-four hours is looking to be among the worst of Kyla's life. Aside from being happy for Jameca, she currently could not find one single thing to be happy about. Her five-year relationship is over in the blink of an eye, her drug addicted brother has now managed to steal from every member of her family, and to add insult to injury, her father doesn't even know who she is. Twenty-five hours ago, she may have felt that life itself is something to be happy about. But tonight, she isn't quite certain.

Kyla drives aimlessly until she pulls up to a bar called Hershey's, that she has seen in passing, but has never been inside. She didn't want to be around anything even remotely familiar. The thought of running into her ex or her friends, makes her feel the worst of anxiety. But she's sure she is safe in this bar that doesn't appear to be the type of establishment that her boogie friends would go to and not nearly enough debauchery for her exhibitionist ex. In fact, the bar is the perfect laid back and peaceful environment for Kyla to sit back and unwind, while listening to music and watching pool table and dart board competitions.

"Can I have a Long Island Iced Tea, please? And keep 'em comin'." Kyla blurts out as she sits down at the bar.

The female bartender returns with her drink, and after a few hours and a few more drinks, Kyla's mind is free from thoughts of the traumatic day she's had. All she can think about is the attractive guy across the room giving her *all* the eyes. He is a little short for her taste, but overall, he's pretty cute. She takes another sip of her drink and smiles in his direction. In an effort to play hard to get, she slowly turns back toward the bar, with deliberate lingering eye contact with her admirer. She can almost count down the seconds in her head before she feels a presence behind her.

"Excuse me?" His voice is unusually deep.

Kyla slowly turns on her stool to make eye contact with the stranger.

"Hello, my name is Mark." He extends his hand.

"Hello Mark. I'm Ky." Kyla tries not to slur her words.

Intoxicated beyond inhibition, Kyla is only concerned with feeling some level of pleasure. In her inebriated state, her judgment is unreliable at best. But she continues her exchange with the handsome stranger, secretly hoping for an experience that will make her feel something more than pain, disappointment, and heartache.

"Can I buy you another drink?" Mark asks.

"Long Island Tea."

"You heard the lady." He tells the bartender.

The bartender takes the order with no regard for how many drinks she has served to one patron already.

"May I?" Mark asks.

Kyla moves her jacket from the stool next to her to allow him to sit.

"So, what is a woman as beautiful as you, doing out alone?"

"Looking for trouble." Kyla dips her index finger in her drink and then sensuously and slowly sucks the dripping liquid from her finger.

"Is that right?" Mark asks, as he uses his eyes to take inventory of Kyla's merchandise.

Beyond the sexy rumble from the bass in his voice, Kyla could care less about what is coming out of his mouth. She is more focused on his eyes, lips, and the muscles rippling through his fitted t-shirt.

"So, where are you from?" Mark continues to try to become acquainted.

"It doesn't matter. You probably won't see me again. Follow me."

With a devilish grin on her face and Mark's collar in her hand, Kyla leads him to the bar's single-occupant restroom. She pulls him in, locking the door behind them. Immediately, Kyla begins to unbuckle Mark's belt.

"Whoa, whoa little lady! You sure this is. . ."

"Shut up!" Kyla kisses him to keep him quiet while she continues to expose his manhood.

After she determines that Mark is worth the indiscretion, she removes a condom from her pouch and proceeds with her alcohol induced one-night stand. Her vibrating phone shows yet another missed call from Arron, which only fuels her need to continue what she has started with Mark. In her drunken state o consciousness and fragile state of heart, Kyla feels somehow that this act of rebellion will make her feel better about the past twenty-four hours. But in reality, allowing this stranger to experience pleasures she feels is meant for the man she loves, only makes her feel worse.

Physically, the pleasure is mind blowing. But every time she closes her eyes, all she sees are images of Arron, Caleb, and her father. Mark releases a deep groan of pleasure as he gives new life to the inside of the condom. Kyla, without hesitating, pulls herself together and leaves the bathroom, leaving Mark standing there with a full condom hanging from the end of his penis. Kyla tips the waitress and leaves the bar before Mark even has the opportunity to exit the bathroom and get her phone number.

For the second day in a row, Kyla wakes up wishing she hadn't. Eyes red and head pounding, she can't recall how she even got home the night before. She slowly sits upright on the couch and lights a much-needed cigarette. As she exhales the first hit like it's a breath of fresh oxygen, she notices a message light blinging on her phone. She expects to see the message from Arron and even scrolls past without reading it. But, the other two messages grab her attention.

The first is a message from her doctor's office, requesting yet again that she come in. However, the second message takes precedence over the others.

(Message) *Ms. LaRue, I tried calling you several times over night and again this morning. Please come to the ICU, your father has had a set-back. Room 420. . . Nurse Nancy.*

Grateful that she gave the hospital permission to text her in the event of an emergency, Kyla gets dressed in record time and heads to the hospital.

She almost wishes she had Arron by her side through all of this. And then, she remembers that Arron is a part of "all of this" and is saddened by the fact that she feels she truly has no one else. Caleb is probably somewhere high out of his mind. Jameca is too wrapped up in herself. And her mom is dead. So, she summons all the strength she can to get through this alone. She hops in the driver's seat of her car and notices a pair of lace boy short underwear on the passenger side floor.

"What the hell?"

Kyla picks up the underwear recognizing them as her own. Confused, she takes a moment to recall events from the night before. Flashes of the bar, and the drinking, then Mark, and then the bathroom, begin to flood her mind all at once. Now, with a sober mind, she remembers her actions and is riddled with shame.

"Oh my God! What in the world did I do?"

# Chapter Six

## "You sneaky little bastard."

       The drive to the hospital is a blur, as her mind is polluted with residual drunken memories from the night before. As she pulls into the parking lot, she ignores another call from Arron. Deciding to deal with the matter at hand, Kyla makes the decision to turn off her phone completely. She enters the elevator with a feeling of numb anxiety and the four-floor elevator ride seems like an eternity. With her mind in a fog and her stomach in knots, she briskly makes her way to ICU room 420.

       She enters to see Caleb hoovering over Theo like a vulture.

"What the hell are you doing here?" She says in a low growl, through clenched teeth. "Didn't I tell you not to come back?"

"Oh yeah!" Caleb chuckles. "I thought I was dreaming."

"Leave Caleb." She raises her voice slightly.

"He's my dad too!" Caleb screams.

"Is he? Or is he your personal ATM machine? How could you steal his money, Caleb? You know what? Don't even answer that. Just leave." Kyla turns her back on Caleb and gives her attention to Theo, who has been placed in a medically induced coma to allow his body to rest.

"Who do you think you are anyway?" Caleb breaks the momentary silence. "You're no better than me. So what, you've got a little money, you're still not happy. You might as well hang out at the dope house with me. Lord knows I see Arron there enough, buying pills."

Surprised by his comment, Kyla's attention is diverted directly to Caleb.

"That's right. You're not hiding from anybody. Your boyfriend's a hype and a whore, your brother's a junky and you think you're a shiny penny in the middle of all the trash?" He mocks. "Hmph, I don't think so. You've got your shit too. Always trying to prove you're everything that you're not, while you step on the little people along the way." He hits a nerve.

"Caleb, get the hell out!"

"Give me fifty bucks and I'll leave." He bargains.

"You've got all the money you'll ever get from me, loser."

"Welp, so be it."

Caleb walks over to the opposite side of Theo's bed and plants a soft kiss on his forehead. "Thanks, old man." He whispers, before leaving the room without another word.

Kyla turns her attention back to Theo. Her heart breaks at how feeble her once strong and able-bodied father looks hooked up to a machine to assist in his breathing.

"Excuse me, Ms. LaRue." Dr. Johnson, Theo's doctor interrupts her assessment.

"Hello Dr. Johnson. I don't understand why he's in ICU. What happened?"

"Please, have a seat."

Kyla sits in the chair next to her father and notices that the $1,500 retirement watch that her dad never removes from his wrist, is missing.

"You sneaky little bastard." She refers to Caleb under her breath.

"I'm sorry?" Dr. Johnson retorts.

"No, not you doctor. I apologize. "

"Well", Dr. Johnson continues. "your father has suffered a massive heart attack. Which is truly trivial considering he doesn't have a history of heart disease. It's almost like. . . like he's psychologically made himself sick physically, if that makes any sense at all. He seems extremely depressed and sad most of the time. Especially when he realizes his wife is not coming to see him; which he seems to have to be reminded of several times a day. When we found him in arrest, he was holding these pictures."

The doctor removes four photos from his lab coat. There was one picture of her at age fourteen, another of Caleb at age ten and two other pictures of her mother and father on their wedding day. She began to reminisce about a time before everything in her life was upside down. And then, with sad eyes Kyla turns her attention toward the doctor.

"Dr. Johnson, do you think my dad will get better?"

"Ms. LaRue, we are running test to see what the medical reason could be for your father's deterioration. We will do everything we can." Dr. Johnson tries to sound reassuring.

Kyla spends the next few hours sitting by her father's bedside or outside in the smoking area. Her thoughts wander from Caleb stealing her dad's watch right in front of her, to the fact that the last time she saw her father, he didn't even know who she was. She feels herself breaking down slowly, but she tries to hold on to her sanity with every fiber.

Before going home for the evening, she is sure to go to security and take the necessary precautions to stop Caleb from coming back into the hospital once and for all. She can't do anything about her father's health, but Kyla is determined to do what she has to do to protect him as best she can.

# Chapter Seven

## "Don't touch me!"

Waking up alone for the second morning in a row, Kyla knows it is going to be a lot to get used to. Without alcohol, she found it difficult to fall asleep the night before, after leaving Theo at the hospital. Her mind refuses to quit. Thoughts and emotions fight to occupy her as she tries to find comfort in her head and in her bed. After hours of struggling to sleep, she finally manages to get a couple of hours of rest.

Ding! Dong!

Kyla is startled awake by the sound of an unexpected visitor.

Ding! Dong!

She struggles to blindly find her slippers with her feet, and then snatches her robe from the back of her bedroom door.

"Who is it?" She asks forcefully.

Irritated by no response, she screams at the silent visitor.

"Who the hell is it?!"

"Babe, it's me."

She immediately recognizes Arron's pleading voice. Hesitantly, she cracks the door to see several dozen roses. In the distance, she sees Arron's pitiful glare through the flowers. A week ago, she may have been impressed, but not today. And it shows all over her face as she rolls her eyes while walking away, leaving Arron standing at the door.

Now upset, he follows her inside, all the way to the kitchen where she prepares her Keurig machine to make a cup of coffee and lights a cigarette.

"I mean damn, I came over here to apologize."

She leans against the counter and tilts her head slightly. "Then apologize."

"I spent all this money on these flowers and shit, and this how you gone act?"

"I'm sorry, is that your apology?" Kyla questions.

"Can you even pretend like you're happy to see me, damn?"

Kyla leans on the counter, waiting on her coffee, puffing her cigarette. She thinks of which issue she wants to address first: Him showing up unannounced. Him acting like flowers are enough to forgive him for the past five years. Or the fact that she should be grateful about it. So, after careful consideration, she decides not to address either.

"Get out. Get out and take your flowers with you." Her tone is even but stern.

"This how you gone do me for real Ky? I just want to come home, baby." He completely changes his attitude.

Kyla grabs her piping hot cup of coffee and slowly walks in Arron's direction.

"THIS is my home. And in case you didn't get the memo, you don't live here anymore."

She continues toward him with her cup held high enough to pour the coffee down his chest, backing him out of the kitchen and into the living room, where she stops and takes a sip of coffee.

"So, my suggestion is that you find you a home of your own. Goodbye."

"You smashin' somebody else, ain't you?"

"What? Boy bye! Why would I give you answers to something that isn't your business? And what difference does it make anyway? Weren't you "smashin'" somebody. . . no, several somebodies, while we were still together? So, don't come to me like that!"

"It's different, cause I'm a man. When you do it, you look like a hoe." Arron's attempt at making sense.

"What the hell did you just say to me?" Kyla's anger has visibly been kindled.

48

"I mean, men and women can't act the same when it comes to sex." Arron tries to clean up his statement.

"What about the part where two people in a relationship only "smash" each other? Huh? How 'bout that?"

Kyla can hear her phone ringing from the bedroom for the second time. She immediately thinks about her father and the hospital, and hurries to her bedroom.

"Hello? . . . Yes, this is she. . . What? No! Please, don't say that!" Kyla drops the phone, falls to her knees, and cries with agonizing pain.

Arron, unsure of what to do, makes and attempt to console her by putting his arm around her.

"Don't touch me!" She screams.

Arron feels it best that he keeps whatever snide comment he is thinking to himself.

Kyla stands and silently dresses in a sweatshirt, jeans, and tennis before leaving the condo and Arron standing cluelessly in the living room.

49

# Chapter Eight

## "What now?"

Her heart is beating fast, but she can barely breathe. As Kyla walks into the St. Louis City Morgue, her stomach plummets and it feels like all the blood has rushed from her head. She looks at the piece of paper with the name of a detective, Detective John Morrison written on it.

She approaches a man that sits at what looks to be a security desk, but he wasn't wearing a uniform. "I'm here to see Detective Morrison."

The man picks up a phone and calls the detective over an intercom.

"Just have a seat. He will be here shortly."

The man points her in the direction of two chairs posing as a sitting area. A minute or two passes before a tall olive-skinned man greets her.

"Ms. LaRue?" He extends his hand.

"Yes." Kyla stands and reciprocates his gesture.

"Right this way." The detective speaks with empathy as he leads Kyla down the long hallway with a light every few feet in the middle of the ceiling. "I know this can be difficult, but I'll be right there with you. We just need a definitive yes or no. Okay?"

"Okay." She says in a whisper.

The longer they walk, it becomes even harder to breath, but all she can think about is smoking a cigarette.

"Just around the corner here." The detective announces.

They stand in front of the large window with the view into a room that contains a man's body lying on a gurney. Kyla immediately looks down at the floor before her eyes focus on the body. She shivers as a knot forms in her throat and tears form in her eyes. She slowly raises her head and focuses her eyes on the lifeless body lying on the cold slab.

"Yes, that's him. That's Caleb LaRue."

Barely able to hold it together, Kyla signs the paperwork to confirm Caleb's identity. She is forced to hear the gruesome details of how Caleb was found to determine if she needs an autopsy. But it is clear to her and the detective that Caleb overdosed. She is given a pawn receipt from his belongings for her dad's watch in the amount of $300.00, but of course no money.

Trying hard to hold in her emotions, Kyla bursts through the doors of the morgue and vomits all over the pavement. She cries as she recalls her last moments with Caleb, and then, she bends over and throws up again. But this time she notices something. She bends down to get a closer look to be sure her eyes aren't deceiving her. Kyla realizes that there is a massive amount of blood in her vomit. She immediately puts her doctor's address into the GPS on her phone. She figures it's time to take that trip to Dr. Okai's office.

Kyla releases a much-needed breath of tension.

"What now?"

# Chapter Nine

## "I should've done something!"

An hour in her doctor's office parking lot passes before she can move. Every time she thinks about her brother, she bursts into tears. They didn't have the best relationship, and deep-down Kyla knows that even though his addiction played a part, she did nothing to improve their relationship. Experiencing an array of emotions; grief, guilt, sadness, relief, and then grief all over again, she finally makes her way out of her car and into the building. She slowly and deliberately walks to her doctor's suite and signs in.

"Hey Linda." Kyla greets the receptionist.

"Oh yes, Ms. LaRue, Dr. Okai will see you as soon as possible." The receptionist says with urgency.

Kyla sits in the waiting room and numbly thumbs through pages of magazines without even focusing. She is numb; all cried out. Thoughts of how she has banned Caleb from the hospital and how now he can't come even if she wants him to, causes her to whimper.

"Kyla LaRue? Dr. Okai will see you now." A new nurse apparently named Jackie, based on her name tag, leads her to a room. "Dr. Okai will be right in. Make yourself comfortable."

Nurse Jackie leaves her alone again with her thoughts. Kyla tries to think back to a time she tried to help Caleb, but all she remembers more rejection, than support.

She cries into her hands. "I should've done something! Anything!"

Knock! Knock! Knock!

The doctor's knock on the door allows her a moment to pull herself together before she enters.

"Hello Ms. LaRue. How are you feeling today?" Dr. Okai asks, as she reviews Kyla's chart.

"I don't really know how to answer that." She sighs. "There's a lot going on right now. But I got concerned today when I vomited blood."

"Was it pure blood, or was it blood in your vomit? And can you recall whether not it was bright red?" The doctor asks with concern.

"It was in my vomit, but it was a lot. And I'm not sure about the color."

"Are you feeling any pain at the moment?"

"No."

"Well, you came in last week because you were feeling a little strange, so you put it. I did a full work up on you as to rule out everything that we would normally run a test for. We first saw abnormal AFP or Alpha-fetoprotein levels. They are high, which indicate signs of trouble with the liver. Since we also did an MRI of your chest and upper abdomen, we were able to determine that you have substantial legions on your lungs and liver. I'm sorry Ms. LaRue, but based on your test results, you have stage-four small cell lung and liver Cancer. We have several methods of treatment that we can explore that may give you the best quality of life."

The doctor's words began to fade to silence as Kyla watches her lips move. She is hoping that she wakes up from this nightmare called her life. She nods as silent tears stream down her face and the feeling of hopelessness washes over her body.

Afraid to ask, she realizes it is imperative and inevitable that she finds out. "How long?"

With her eyes closes, Kyla listens as Dr. Okai administers the final blow.

"Four to six months. . . at the most."

# Chapter Ten

## "I miss you so much."

It has been two days since identifying her brother's body and learning of her own Cancer diagnosis. She has not been to work. She can't find the strength to go to the hospital to see her father. And she does not want to communicate with the outside world. Kyla remembers a time when she would combat these emotions by writing. At age fourteen, she began to journal almost everything she thought, felt, or did. In her twenties, her writing began to taper off a bit. But by the time she had been with Arron for a couple of years, she stopped altogether. Plus, she doesn't even think she can find the words right now.

Realizing it is her responsibility to arrange Caleb's services, Kyla scrolls through her contacts to give herself an idea of how many people she will need to get in touch with. While scrolling, she comes to a name that warms her soul and puts a smile on her face even with all she's going through, Aunt Ce Ce.

Celeste LaRue is Theo's younger sister and Kyla's favorite aunt. Originally from New Orleans, along with Theo, Celeste is as creole as they come. She moved to St. Louis after hurricane Katrina and has lived here ever since. She is the one-person Kyla feels she can talk to right now. In fact, Kyla has been so wrapped up in her own life, she hasn't been to see her aunt in almost a year. But she knows that she needs someone right now. Someone that she knows loves her more than anything. So, she sets out to pay Aunt Ce Ce a visit.

Almost an hour later, Kyla drives down the long gravel driveway leading to the large secluded plantation style home. In the distance, she can already see her aunt perched on the huge wooden front porch.

Upon noticing an unidentified vehicle approaching, Celeste halts the rocking in her chair and sits still as if to camouflage herself in her surroundings. Once Kyla's vehicle approaches the house, Celeste instantly recognizes her favorite niece and hurriedly heads for the car.

"Kay Kay!" Celeste gleefully shouts as she sprints toward Kyla with open arms.

"Aunt Ce Ce!"

The two women embrace firmly and hold on as if they will never let go, while Kyla forces back tears.

"To what do I owe this pleasure?" Celeste asks in her rich creole accent, as she escorts Kyla onto the porch and into the house.

Kyla has never realized until today how much she favors Celeste and it warms her heart.

"I'm ashamed to say that it's not because it just crossed my mind to visit, although I am extremely happy to see you."

They sit next to one another on the elegant living room sofa and Kyla places her hands over her aunt's and looks intensely into her eyes.

"Tee Tee, I want to sincerely apologize for not coming to see you sooner. I just have so much going on."

"Girl please. I am absolutely fine. I don't come to see you either. I'm just not privy to all that fast city living. I like the peaceful atmosphere of the country. That's what I miss about New Orleans." She begins to reminisce. "But a phone call or two every now and then, wouldn't hurt."

"I miss you so much." Kyla's proclamation sounds more like a heart-felt confession.

"I miss you, *Mon Coeur*. I miss that beautiful voice too."

Kyla can't remember the last time someone inquired about her singing or the last time she heard those words come from her sweet aunt's lips. . . *My Heart*. As the words cause her to think about her past life, her heart begins to break. She hasn't even scratched the surface of why she came to visit and she's already afraid to say another word. But she knows it is unavoidable.

"My dad is in the hospital." Kyla says without thinking. "He had a heart attack and is in the ICU."

"Oh my! How are you kids holding up?"

Before she is able to contain another ounce of grief, Kyla breaks down into frantic tears into Celeste's lap.

"Oh there, there honey. Let it out." Celeste rubs Kyla's back and shoulders tenderly and allow her to release her emotions.

After a few minutes of unbridled tears, Kyla is finally able to speak once again.

"Caleb died of an overdose two days ago." This time Kyla sits silently and allow the tears to flow.

"My God! Is that what caused Theo's heart attack?"

"No ma'am. Daddy doesn't even know that he's is gone. He's been in a coma since the day before Caleb died."

"How long has my brother been sick?" Celeste is curt.

"That's the thing Tee Tee, he wasn't. I mean, he fell and had to go into therapy, but heart attack sick. . . no way! His doctor isn't even sure of the cause. He just stares at pictures of Momma and he doesn't even know who I am half the time anymore."

"*Gen maldamou.*" Celeste says.

"What does that mean?"

Celeste stands and walks up to the mantel and admires a wedding photo of Theo and Shilynne.

"It means, he has a broken heart." Celeste is saddened. "For that, there is no cure; only time."

Celeste turns to face Kyla and searches for her eyes until she finds them.

"What else?" She asks Kyla.

"What do you mean?"

"I mean child, that there is something else that you're holding on to. I see it in your eyes. You have not completely freed your soul."

63

Kyla remembers that even as a child, she could keep almost nothing from Aunt Ce Ce. It is almost as if she has an eye into her soul.

Celeste returns to her seat next to Kyla. But this time, she holds Kyla's hands inside of hers.

"Speak child." She insists.

She doesn't know if it's the sincerity in her voice or the Cajun accent, but like always, Kyla finds herself baring her soul to Celeste.

"I have stage-four lung and liver Cancer. Wow! I think that's the first time I said it out loud."

"Watch your mouth! You have only been diagnosed; you do not HAVE anything. Kyla, your body must line up with your spirit. But first, you must get your spirit properly aligned. You are all over the place."

Kyla knows that her aunt is speaking wisdom, but right now her mind is not in the place to receive it.

"May I pray with you, *Mon Coeur*?"

"Yes ma'am."

Prayer has never been Kyla's thing, but Celeste has always made her remember that there is a spiritual side to life. Although, the concept of it all goes completely over her head. Nevertheless, she allows her aunt to pray over her and anoint her with oil. When she can tune out her own thoughts long enough, she hears Celeste say things like, "physician heal thyself" and how God is strength in our weakness. But Kyla is too impacted by grief and self-pity to absorb a thing. After prayer, Celeste gives Kyla the name and address to a place she feels will help her niece.

"Here. Go here, tomorrow night and sit with these people."

Kyla looks at the paper with suspicion. "The Kingdom House? Tee Tee what's this?"

"They can help you get through what you're dealing with. In the meantime, you and I will deal with the family stuff together."

"Thank you, Aunt Ce Ce! I don't know what I would do without you right now. "

"Me neither child, me neither."

# Chapter Eleven

## "Please help me!"

Kyla had little experience with going to church as an adult. But she trusts Celeste and with all she's dealing with, she figures going to a church can hardly worsen her situation. Upon arrival, she hadn't expected to see so many people at church on a Thursday night. She stands in the back of the building wearing a scarf and dark shades. There are worse places she can be caught visiting, but she stills feels the need to hide her identity from the congregation. Finding a spot in the last pew, she feels comfortable knowing that no one besides the people in the last row can see her. After she confirms that she doesn't recognize anyone, she settles into her seat and attempts to listen.

"Today I want to talk to the congregation about power. P-O-W-E-R, Persisting Onward with Everlasting Resilience!" The tall, slim, middle-aged Black preacher pauses to allow the congregation's reaction to subside. "Now understand, this is not to negate the power of God. In fact, this is the power that we have inherited from Him. The power that our faith gives us access to. God has given us power over every area of our lives. How we choose to use that power is a different story altogether.

Okay, let me slow it down for yawl. Acts 1:8 tells us, 'You will receive power when the Holy Spirit has come to you.' And this is absolutely true. But I want to take you back to the Old Testament. Proverbs 18:21 says, 'Death and life are in the power of the tongue: and they that love it shall eat the fruit thereof.' Now, the tongue is just one member. However, through our creator we have power over every member and every area of our lives. According to the word, our tongue has the power to destroy and sustain. But the key to this power is rooted in our faith in God. Hebrews 11:1 tells us, 'Now faith is the substance of things hoped for, the evidence of things not seen.' Faith is not to be taken for granted!

All of the things that we seek God for, he has given us the power through in Him, to perform. Healing, prosperity, blessings, relationships. . . He has equipped us with the power to deal with these things. These are Kingdom principles. To someone without faith, I know this has to sound like some type of fairy tale. But because I have operated in this power and I have witnessed what God is capable of first hand, I know these things to be true. There is nothing special about me except for my undying faith in God and my desire to seek His Will for my life. It has been the best journey I have ever been on! Hallelujah!

P-O-W-E-R, Persisting Onward with Everlasting Resilience! See saints, my job is not to hold you hostage and force you into a relationship with your heavenly Father. It is my job however, to equip you with what you need to develop that relationship. You must walk into your inheritance of POWER."

The music begins to play softly, and the choir hums the hymn as the preacher begins to invite attendees to the alter for prayer.

"Talk to him. Ask Him what he would have you to do with the life he has afforded you. Ask Him for guidance. Ask Him for healing of whatever is ailing you. Talk to Him about your sorrows. Open up about your feelings of rejection and depression. And when you do, have the faith that it takes to activate the power you need to make a change. We are open if you need prayer, please come forward. But I need you to know that when you leave, God is still listening. Yeshua is still your savior, receive him, receive love, receive true POWER."

Kyla quietly slides out of her pew and into the back of the church. She stands for a moment and takes notice of the people surrendering to an invisible entity. The message is uplifting, she must admit, but she is not ready to be as transparent as many others in the room.

On the way out, a bulletin board with event and meeting flyers catches her attention. A 'Faith for

Survival' support group flyer jumps out at her. Kyla looks around and quickly takes a picture of the flyer and makes it her screensaver before disappearing out the front door.

The trip home is silent. Instead of music, Kyla wants to be alone with *her* thoughts; *her* reality. Not the reality of a fictional situation created by the lyrics of a song, or the reality of the news of some celebrity or stranger. She wants to ponder the non-self-perceived reality of her LIFE. As she drives in silence she begins to think.

*"My baby brother is dead, and our last interaction was hateful at best. To be honest, I haven't really been much of a big sister since he was about eight-years-old. My dad is in a coma, from an unexplained heart attack. I love my dad, but deep down I think I feel like he deserves what he's going through because of who he was in the past. And my poor mother, she didn't deserve anything she endured. . . "*

She begins to think about who she is when no one is looking. The alcohol, the occasional use of pills, the casual sex, the greed, the envious behavior, her pride. She feels like the poster child for the seven deadly sins.

Kyla begins to cry uncontrollably. Feeling unsafe to drive, she pulls the car over to the side of the road and turns on her hazard lights. As if to mimic her emotions, it has begun to rain. Tears pouring down her cheeks to rival the rain on her windshield, Kyla feels the weight of every secret, every indiscretion, and every regret, and she makes an attempt to pray to a God she isn't sure exists, about a faith she isn't even sure she can obtain.

"God, I don't even know if you can hear someone like me, but if you're real, I really need you right now." Her prayer is so inaudible through her sobs, only God can understand her. "Please help me. . . he. . . heal me!"

# Chapter Twelve

## "Everything I touch turns to crap!"

A cigarette burns in the ashtray like incense while Kyla sits with her knees to her chest on the sofa. The support group flyer taunts her from her phone across the table, and she finally retrieves it. After last night's breakdown, she feels exposed to an entity that knows her better than she knows herself. Not yet willing to admit it to anyone, not even herself, she feels that something has changed within her. Looking over the flyer, Kyla notices several scriptures that catch her attention. James 5:14, Isaiah 53:5, 1 Peter 2:24, Matthew 17:20, and Hebrew 11:11. She downloads an app that allows her to pull up the verses on her phone. She begins to read about faith and healing, and she decides to go to the support group that evening. With much on her agenda for the day, she decides to visit Theo before heading to the funeral home to finalize Caleb's arrangements.

As Kyla rides through St. Louis City, she takes notice of children running, laughing, and playing; things she never takes time to notice. The realization that she will never have children of her own hits her like a ton of bricks, and a single tear escapes her eye. She never even realized that the possibility is so important, until there is none. Emotions are running high and that makes her angry. Since she was a teenager, Kyla prides herself on being less emotional than the "average" woman. But today, the reality of the things she will never have the opportunity to experience, come to the forefront all at once. She will never get married, or give birth, or really truly fall in love, for that matter.

The inconsolable thought causes her to pull over to the side of the road. She's tired of crying. She's tired of not being in control of her own emotions. Kyla grips the steering wheel as if it is the life-support she needs to overcome the attack of emotion that she is

73

experiencing. Tears and snot cover her face before she is finally able to slow her breathing and avoid a full-fledged anxiety attack. Just as she begins to calm herself, her cell phone rings. She picks up the phone to see Arron calling, which only enrages her causing her to throw the phone across the car as she releases a scream of anguish mixed with anger.

She can see that the screen on her phone is cracked from across the car. And then, she begins to laugh hysterically.

"Everything I touch turns to crap!"

Looking around to realize she is not in the most-savory of neighborhoods, she snaps out of her hysterics and pulls off. Although, she feels a slight headache trying to surface, Kyla actually feels a little better; like a weight has been lifted. Having had her moment, she continues on to the hospital to visit her father.

Upon arrival to the hospital, Kyla notices that Theo no longer has tubes in his nose and mouth. A young nurse that walks in to check the levels of the IV fluids, notices Kyla sitting in a chair in the corner of the room.

"He's doing pretty good today! He was breathing over the machine, so we took him off. He hasn't had any issues." The nurse informs Kyla.

"That's great." Kyla says dryly.

"Okay, well let me know if you need anything." The nurse senses Kyla's desire to be alone.

From across the room, Kyla watches her father's chest rise and fall with every breath. And then, she thinks about the inevitability of that breath ceasing to exist. Feeling the cloud of agony approaching, she retreats to her father's side and grabs his hand.

"Hi Daddy. I don't know if you can even feel or hear me, but I have some things to tell you." A knot of emotion forms in her throat. "Caleb's gone Daddy, and I'm sick. So, you see, you've got to get better. You and Aunt Ce Ce can live in that big ole house together and take care of each other, like brothers and sisters should." Her voice tapers off at the thought of her inability to take care of her own brother.

"Shilynne?" Theo whispers.

Kyla is so caught up in her own grief, she doesn't notice Theo watching her.

"Daddy, it's me, Kyla."

"You sure look like my Shilynne. I'm gonna ask her to marry me, you know." He smiles.

With no energy to combat Theo's dementia, Kyla listens as her father revisits a time before she even existed.

"Yes, I bet she'll be a beautiful bride." Kyla agrees.

Theo speaks in a whisper until he falls back into a deep sleep. Kyla kisses her father's forehead and continues on her journey to the support group.

Apprehension sets in when Kyla pulls up to the church. She can recall the very real emotions she has been experiencing since she last visited. When she walks in, she can hear several voices chattering and follows the sound until she sees a group of people containing four women and two men.

"Hi, is this the. . . Faith for Survival support group?" Kyla asks, taking a peek at her phone.

A woman that is extremely familiar to Kyla approaches.

"Yes, it is! We're very delighted to have you. My name is Heaven." The woman embraces Kyla. "This is Trish, Chuck, Greg, Valerie, and Juliet."

"I'm Kyla. I apologize in advance, I won't remember anyone's name." And nor will she try.

She has been in the room for sixty-seconds and she already can't wait until it's over so she can leave.

"So, are you a survivor or are you here for a loved one?" Heaven asks.

"Well, I'm dying of Cancer. I'd hardly call that surviving." Kyla snaps. "I'm sorry, maybe I should try this some other time."

Kyla heads toward the exit but is stopped by Heaven. "Wait! Please stay. Trust me, I know exactly how you feel. Before I started this group, I was just like you. Give it a chance."

Kyla looks at Heaven from head to toe. "Well, you don't seem to be suffering from two forms of stage-four Cancer either."

"You're right. But I was diagnosed with terminal stage-four brain Cancer. . . three years ago."

Kyla looks at a healthy Heaven as she leaves Kyla standing at the door and returns to the group. Partially offended and astonished, she reluctantly makes her way back into the room. Aside from the fact that Heaven shows no signs of being sick, Kyla can't get over the feeling that she knows her from somewhere, so she stares without even realizing it.

"She's amazing, isn't she?" Trish asks, noticing Kyla's stare.

"Um, yes. I suppose she is. So, is she Cancer free?"

"Yep! She's been in remission for two years. Everyone is still in amazement. I'm still praying for that kind of faith and healing."

Kyla turns her attention to Trish, who is clearly suffering from a terminal illness. Her pale skin is as thin as her hair, but her sunken eyes still show a glimmer of hope.

"Yeah, me too." Kyla says.

Making her way to a group of chairs arranged in a circle, Kyla sits alone as she watches a few more people make an entrance and socialize with the existing few attendees. After a few minutes, everyone begins to take their seat, and Heaven takes the floor.

"Welcome everyone! I would like to thank you all for coming out another week to support one another!"

Heaven begins with a prayer that allows Kyla to take note of all the attendees without their knowledge. Kyla looks around the room at the sick people with hopeful faces. All except for a few are riddled with fragile bodies and thinning hair.

"Amen." Everyone says in unison.

"We have someone new joining us today. But first, we will pick up where we left off last week and allow our guest to get comfortable. Did everyone bring their journals?"

All those that possess a journal, hold them in the air.

"Okay great!" Heaven continues. "Howard, we left off last week with you sharing how journaling is helping you to cope with your diagnosis."

Howard, a middle-aged Black man, scoots to the edge of his seat to avoid standing and exerting more strength and energy than is necessary.

"Hi everybody. For those of you who don't know me, I'm Howard and I've been diagnosed with stage-three prostate Cancer. I've been getting treatment for about two months now and I have to admit I am the weakest I've ever been in my life, and I don't like it. But I hold on to the fact that I'm still alive to fight this fight. Honestly, I wasn't taking to this journaling thing at first. But, when my wife left me after I was diagnosed, I thought I wouldn't make it another day. God has shown me where my help, my faith, and my strength lies. Journaling for me has been about reflection and coming to terms with my past, while allowing me to accept the fate of my future; whatever that may be. So, I just wanna say, I thank God that I'm here and I'm believing God for my healing. Thank you, guys." Howard waves one hand and slides back in his chair.

"Thank you, Howard." Heaven says. "Would anyone else care to share?"

Watching Heaven's every move, Kyla racks her brain to remember where she knows her from. She's younger than Kyla, but she figures she seems much too classy to have dated Caleb. Interrupting her thoughts, Valerie stands and begins to speak. Kyla is taken aback by how frail her body is as she speaks like the wind has been knocked out of her.

"Hello everyone." Valerie takes a seat before she continues. "As you all know, I've been on this bout with breast Cancer for five years. I've experienced every high and every low, and journaling has helped me to rejoice during the highs and cope through the lows. But the past month has been difficult, so I started recording myself, and I really like it. It gives me something to leave to my children when I'm gone. I know that seems morbid, but it gives me peace. I've really appreciated this group and the things I've learned about how important my presence is to making history. How every connection has the capacity to change a multitude of lives, and I believe that because of this group, God has allowed me to do this." A tear escapes her eye as she continues to speak. "Today will be my last day in group. I'm being placed on hospice."

A series of gasps and groans of disappointment can be heard, followed by a few women sobbing quietly.

"It's okay. I'm okay. This life has been wonderful! Meeting you all has been a beautiful and humbling experience. When I was diagnosed five years ago, the doctors gave me six months, but God has given me four and a half more years. Four and a half years to touch people's lives, to love my husband, to pour into my children, and to do things I never would have done had I not been diagnosed. So, although I will never stop believing God for complete healing, I am grateful for every second he gives me. Thank you all."

A very distraught woman walks out of the room and others go over to console Valerie. Meanwhile,

Heaven watches Kyla's observations of everyone else. The room settles down and Heaven takes the floor again.

"So, as you all can see we have visitor today. Her name is Kyla. Would you like to share anything with the group?"

Kyla looks at every individual face and feels she has nothing to complain about in this moment. In fact, after hearing the others speak, she is almost ashamed of her attitude upon arrival. Her emotions are so mixed, she doesn't know whether to break down or lash out.

"No, thank you. I'm good." She lies.

"Okay then. No worries. Everyone, please socialize with one another. There are snacks in the back. I'll be available for prayer or counseling until the session is over. I would like to close by thanking God for allowing us this time together and remember, God has given us the power to make our bodies line up with our spirit, so heal your spirit first."

The group mingles for a few moments before Kyla makes her way to speak with Heaven.

"I want to apologize for my rudeness earlier. I got diagnosed very recently and I'm still having a hard time." Kyla says with sincerity.

"No need to apologize. I completely understand." Heaven places her hand on Kyla's shoulder and tilts her head to one side.

"You don't remember me, do you?"

Before Kyla can respond, an interruption from a man not a part of the support group, invokes a jolt in her memory.

"You ready?" The tall and handsome intruder asks Heaven.

"Donovan?" Kyla immediately recognizes him.

Now Kyla remembers. Donovan King, a former classmate, was once a short and scrawny outcast of the "popular kids", but still cute enough for Kyla to have a secret crush, despite her treatment of him. And Heaven, just happens to be his twin sister. She admires Donovan and his metamorphosis into an absolutely gorgeous specimen of a man; clean cut, caramel skin, muscular build, seductive brown eyes, and a chiseled jawline. She takes him all in.

Donovan briefly searches his own memory and recognizes her immediately. "Kyla!"

The two smile and give one another a short embrace.

"Yes, I absolutely remember you now!" Kyla says, answering Heaven's earlier question. "Oh wow, it's really good to see you both." Kyla turns to hug Heaven as well. "Now I'm really sorry for how I acted."

"That's perfectly alright, considering." Heaven says, placing her hand on Kyla's shoulder. "So, will you be coming back?"

Kyla throws an innocent smile in Donovan's direction.

"Yes. . . I think I will."

# Chapter Thirteen

## *"God. . .Please don't let me die."*

Running into Donovan the day before throws Kyla for a loop. Here she is, dying from a terminal illness and grieving for her brother, yet she is elated to see how much Donovan has morphed into a beautiful butterfly. And then, she hopes he doesn't remember the way she treated him as a caterpillar. Nevertheless, she's happy to have the chance to see him again.

Since Caleb's funeral arrangements have been finalized, Kyla feels the need to tie up other loose end in her life; namely Arron. She is over his attempts to contact her and decides to block him on all forms of communication. Even changing the locks to her home in the process. Before, the thought of him heartbroken and begging, was flattering. But in reality, she is as done as an overcooked turkey.

The support group meeting leaves her with a lot on her mind and even more on her heart. In fact, reflection seems to have become a major theme in her life. The impact of recent life's events causes her to take a closer look at the person she has become. And even more important, why. In compliance with the group's activity, Kyla bought a journal to begin her reflective journey. She's not quite sure what purpose it serves at this point, but she is willing to explore.

She carries the journal with her everywhere she goes. Even when she visits her now completely unresponsive father in the hospital, she sits in the chair next to his bed staring at blank pages. The more she thinks about what she should write, the more depressed she becomes at her present reality. Slamming the empty journal closed in frustration, Kyla leaves the hospital room without even a glance in her father's direction.

Kyla makes it home in record time. She makes her way to a closet where she stores nostalgic items. After pulling out almost half the closet's contents, she finally finds what she is looking for. The heavy chest is covered with dust and filled with memories. She drags the chest into the middle of the living room floor and dials in the combination. She opens it to reveal almost twenty-years' worth of journals. Bothered by her inability to start writing, Kyla figures she will get inspiration from herself.

She thumbs through the tattered pages and smiles at the recognition of her own handwriting. Each book has a different color and design and is labeled with the month and year, while each page identifies the entries down to the day. Picking up a random journal to read, Kyla reads a page marked May 2nd, twenty years prior. The first sentence on the page makes her immediately recall the incidents of that day.

*So, today has to be the worst day of my life so far...*

*Twenty Years Ago – Kyla Age Sixteen*

She was bored out of her mind, but she knew her mom wouldn't allow her to do what she really wanted to do, smoke a joint. Kyla had gotten busted smoking marijuana only a month before and Shilynne has had a tight leash on her ever since, cutting her off from those she deemed toxic in Kyla's life. However, she still managed to maintain her relationship with Micah. Micah was Kyla's colorful, bi-sexual neighbor and friend. She smoked too, but she was aspiring to go to college and her mom saw Micah as a positive influence. It also helped that Shilynne had no idea that Micah indulged in smoking marijuana.

Feeling secure that her mom would say yes, Kyla got permission to visit Micah. To her satisfaction, Micah was strapped with a joint and they posted up on her back patio. She was only there five minutes when she received a call from a friend that Shilynne had serious reservations about, Andrea.

"What's up girl?" Kyla answered her phone.

"Where you at?!" Andrea asked with urgency.

"Why? What's going on?"

*"Girl! So, you remember Chloe was bullying Erica, right? Well, now she playin' on her phone and threatening her and stuff. Her grandma even playin' on the phone girl! We finna go to her house!"*

*Although Micah was young, Kyla knew that she would have no parts of the nonsense taking place. Not to mention, Kyla didn't want to be talked out of what she was about to do. So, she casually walked to the front of the house before she continued her conversation.*

*"Come get me." She whispered, as she watched for Micah.*

*"Okay, I'm on my way!"*

*Andrea hung up without saying goodbye. In the meantime, Kyla returned as casually to the patio as she left.*

*"What was that about?" Micah asked as she passed Kyla the remainder of the joint.*

*"Aw, nothin'. Andrea just want me to ride with her somewhere."*

*"Hmph."*

"What?" Kyla's guilty curiosity got the best of her. "You got a problem with me hanging Andrea now? First, it was Jameca, now Drea?"

"All I know is, I'm not lying to your mom if she comes over here looking for you. And you know she will."

"Whatever!"

Kyla proceeded to the front of the house where she decided to wait on Andrea alone. She knew Micah was wise beyond her years, but she had to go, and she wasn't even sure why. It was only a few minutes before Andrea arrived, and Kyla rode off into the night.

"We finna ride on these hoes!" Andrea's adrenaline-fueled excitement was contagious.

"Now what happened?"

"They keep talking shit about Erica and trying to punk her, and you know she don't mess with nobody. It's some more people meetin' us over there though."

"Where's Erica?"

*"She gone meet us down the street from Chloe's house. But I gotta stop by my house to pick up Shon."*

*Shon was Andrea's cousin that was always down for some drama. When they pulled up to Andrea's house, her mother was standing on the porch with Shon. Kyla felt a tinge of relief at the thought that someone may actually be about to stop what she felt deep down was a serious mistake.*

*"Where yawl about to go?" Andrea's mother asked.*

*Shon interjected. "I told her we was about to go get with these broads!"*

*"Who else goin' wit yawl?"*

*To Kyla's surprise, Andrea's mother seemed intrigued by the whole situation. She seemed to be living vicariously through them as she orchestrated who would be riding with whom, and even offering to chauffeur a few teens to the battle.*

*By the time the troops had been completely rallied, there were about eight girls and five boys* gathered to participate in the anticipated brawl. Kyla felt a strange nervous anticipation. She thought, 'I can beat them down, and get dropped off at Micah's house before my parents even know I'm gone.'

The energy in all three cars was tremendous. Teenagers yelling and cussing about what they plan to do to the people waiting for them, on their own turf. When they pulled onto the street, only a few people could be seen standing on the porch. Kyla, among the first to jump out of the vehicles, rushed toward the house to find her first victim. Andrea attempted to make her exit from the car.

"Stay in this car!" Andrea's mother yelled.

"But Momma."

"But nothing! Didn't these people already beat yo' ass once?" She reminded Andrea.

Andrea was upset, but she complied with her mother and sat back in the seat with her arms folded across her chest, as she watched helplessly.

Soon after Kyla, teenagers from the other vehicles ran toward the house, resembling gladiators

93

*going to battle. Before they even realized what was happening, teenagers and adults alike from the opposing side, began to run out from the darkness, some with weapons and some without. Some retreated from inside the house and others seemed to be camouflaged between the houses. Kyla and her crew were clearly outnumbered.*

*Kyla charged toward Chloe to assist Erica, the reason for all the drama. She trampled in their direction, resembling a charging bull in her intentions. With balled up fists, Kyla reared her arm to deliver a devastating blow. But, before she could connect, Chloe's brother, Chris, punched Kyla in the face so hard that she saw stars and fell to the ground. As she struggled to get back to her feet, the commotion seemed to move in slow motion and the sound was muffled. Kyla finally steadied herself and was able to get her eyesight in focus. Before she could determine what to do next, she was met with a blow to the head with a metal bat. Again, she found herself down.*

*Dizzy once again, she fought the heaviness of her limbs and began to run in the direction of the car. Adrenaline caused her face to become numb.*

"Oh my God!" Andrea screamed with horror.

Her mother's face was etched with the same terror in Andrea's voice. Before she had the chance to inquire about their reactions, she saw one drop, and then two. And suddenly, a rush of blood began to seep into her eyes. Before long, her head is bleeding profusely, and her face is covered in blood.

First, she thought she'd be able to fight and get back to Micah's before anyone found out. But now, she'd rather die than have to face her mother.

"Them bitches!" Kyla screamed. "Who was that old lady that hit me?"

"Chloe's grandma. I told you she was in it too. Oh my God, Kyla. Your head is bleeding bad!" Andrea said with sheer concern.

On the way back to Andrea's house, Kyla held her head in her hands, hoping not to bleed out.

"If I don't die in this back seat, my momma gone kill me anyway." Kyla said to herself.

"Yo momma gone be too worried to be mad at you."

95

*Kyla lifted her eyes slightly to look at Andrea's mother through bloody hands. "You don't know my momma."*

*Kyla began to whisper. "God please don't let me die like this, please don't let me die."*

*Once they arrived, they hurried inside and attempted to stop the bleeding, while others from the fight started to show up. The conversations ranged from how many unexpected adults ran out of the darkness, to the weapons they possessed.*

*"Girl, we ran to the car when that man pulled out a gun!" One girl exclaimed.*

*Meanwhile, Kyla, Andrea, and her mother, soaked multiple towels trying to stop Kyla's head from bleeding.*

*Finally, Kyla was defeated by her injury. "Call my momma."*

*Those three words alone caused Kyla to burst in to uncontrollable tears.*

*"She gone be so mad at me!"*

As Kyla thinks back to that night she spent in the emergency room with her mom and every lesson she learned, what she remembers most is how it felt to disappoint her mother. She remembers the anger, disappointment, and worry expressed by her mother that day. And then, she rubs the scar that she has worn on her forehead as a badge of stupidity for the past twenty years. As if it can make a difference, her reflection compels her to jot a note in the top left corner of the page, to her sixteen-year-old self.

Ky,

This is one of the stupidest things you've ever done. NEVER GO TO SOMEONE'S HOUSE TO FIGHT. You might wind up dead! But we learned that the hard way, didn't we? Really should've stayed at Micah's.

# Chapter Fourteen

## "What the. . .?"

Saturday mornings are usually dedicated to visiting Theo, but today is different. Kyla feels she must finish tying up those loose ends. Besides Celeste and the support group, no one knows about her diagnosis. So, Jameca is the next on her list to tell. She looks at the open chest as she heads to the bathroom and she remembers her attempt at journaling the night before. After reading an entry from her old journals, she manages to write about her experience at the support group, her feelings about losing Caleb and her dad's illness. The feeling of defeat begins to dissipate somewhat.

Kyla makes her way to the bathroom to perform her morning ritual of facial inventory. Sometimes it is the only way to remember her mother's face without looking at pictures. Her eyes, her nose, her hair, her scar. . . where is her scar? She lifts her hair back further in search of the scar she received twenty-years earlier. She can't understand. In her delirious confusion, she checks the other side of her head to find nothing.

"What the. . .?"

Every day for the past two decades, Kyla has looked in the mirror at that scar. It is a part of her; a part of who she is. . . and now it's gone! In a frenzy, she retrieves her cell phone and turns on the flashlight in order to get a better look at her forehead.

"Where is it?" She says, under her breath.

Suddenly, flashes of memories unexperienced, play in her mind; a flash of seeing the note being burned into the corner of the page twenty years ago, that she left in her childhood journal only the night before. And even more trivial, the memories of the fight begin to fade into background and are overshadowed by memories of her staying at Micah's that night. And then as suddenly as the flashes begin, they stop.

"Oh my God, I'm losing my mind!"

She stands in the mirror holding her face, confused and questioning her own sanity, while her mind holds two different recollections of her reality, but her body only shows evidence or lack thereof, of only one. Kyla feverishly searches her chest for old pictures that expose her forehead. But to her dismay, none of them reveal the scar. It is like it never existed. Realizing she's running late to meet Jameca, Kyla hurriedly showers and dresses to head to the bridal shop. But, not before grabbing her journal on the way out of the door.

Kyla pulls into the almost empty parking lot. She has to check the time to be sure she hasn't arrived too early. It's 2:00 pm on the dot when Jameca pulls up next to her right on cue. The two exit their vehicles and admire the elegant bridal boutique as they approach.

"This is beautiful!" Kyla is taken with the ambiance. "Where's everyone else?"

"It's just me and you today Ky. I don't want everyone's opinion on my dress. And don't think it's anybody's business what your dress looks like. See, I figure, once you choose your dress, I will have that one removed from the bridesmaid's options to choose from. I think it'll keep down confusion. Don't you?"

"I guess." Kyla is unenthusiastic.

She becomes saddened by the thought of the conversation she must have with her friend.

They enter the shop and are immediately greeted by an extremely polite older Haitian woman. Jameca and the woman embrace like old friends.

"Byen venu, my niece!"

"Thank you, Auntie! Aunt Rosaline, this is my Maiden of Honor, Kyla. Kyla, this is my Auntie Rosaline."

"Hello Ms. Rosaline. It's nice to meet you."

Kyla extends her hand, but Rosaline pushes it to the side and embraces her without warning.

"If you are in my Meka's wedding, then you are family." Rosaline says as she releases her. "Would you ladies like some Cremasse?"

"Oooh, yes please!" Jameca exclaims.

"I'm not sure what that is." Kyla says.

"It's a popular Haitian drink. Just try it. Bring her one too, Auntie Rosie. "

"Okay. Be right back!"

Kyla is smitten with Rosaline's Haitian accent. In a way, she reminds her of Aunt Celeste.

"So, your aunt owns the boutique, huh? Why doesn't that surprise me?"

"Because you know I can't deal with everybody."

The two, sit silently for an awkward twenty seconds or so, and then they both attempt to speak at the same time.

"You first." Kyla says.

"Well, I just want to know how you've been since, you know, Caleb. You haven't talked about it much."

"Maybe I'll be able to open up more after his services. I just really don't want to think about it anymore than I have to. You know?"

Jameca nods her head with understanding.

"I do need to talk to you about something, though." Kyla tells her.

Kyla finds it difficult to make eye contact with Jameca.

"Here you go ladies." Rosaline says, as she returns with the Cremasse. "You ready to look at some dresses?"

The usually inattentive Jameca, notices Kyla's seriousness. "Auntie, give us a minute please."

Rosaline leaves the room and all of Jameca's attention is on Kyla.

"What's going on Ky?" Jameca can tell something is more off with Kyla than usual.

"I don't think I'm going to be able to be in your wedding. Well, I mean, I can't be in your wedding."

Jameca, waiting for a reasonable explanation, sits silently and allows Kyla to finish. Kyla finally gives her eye contact and continues to explain why she has to disappoint her friend on her wedding day.

"Jameca, I have Can. . . I mean, I have been diagnosed with Cancer, and the doctors don't expect me to make it until August."

Kyla is barely able to finish her sentence before becoming choked up at the reality that she may not be alive to see another year.

"Cancer? What kind? Have you started treatment? What's your regimen? Oh my God, Kyla!" Jameca begins to breakdown and hyperventilate.

"I know it's a lot but calm down before you pass out."

She grabs Jameca's shoulders and forces her to calm her breathing while she continues.

"Now, to answer your questions, it's lung and liver Cancer. I have not started treatment yet, but we have discussed beginning radiation over the next week."

By the time she finishes, Jameca has calmed down only slightly. But Kyla can see that she is still on the verge of an emotional eruption.

"I really need you right now, Meke."

Silent tears stream down Jameca's face as she nods with empathy. "I'm so sorry."

"It's not your fault." Kyla assures her.

Jameca looks deeply and sincerely into Kyla's eyes before she speaks. "You don't understand. All of these years, everything I've done, has been to compete with or to attempt to be as good as or better than you. When Jeff proposed, the first thing I thought was, 'Hah! She won't get married before me!' But truthfully, he only proposed because I found out he was sleeping with my cousin."

"Oh my God, Meke! Why didn't you tell me?" Kyla is shocked.

"What? So, you can know the truth? Jeff is just a man that makes mistakes too? Never! So, you see, things are not always as perfect as I make them out to be. The hard truth is, I owe all that I am to you. I only strived to be great, because I knew you would be. I never knew why you quit singing, but when you double-majored in finance and psychology, I knew I had to do something amazing! So, I became a doctor. You know me, I wanted to background dance in Aaliyah videos, remember? But now. . . this? I would have never thought that my silent competition would end so soon. I don't know what I'm going to do without you. I know I'm not always the best friend to you, but I can say that you are a great friend to me. You tolerate me when no one else will and you cuss me out when no one else will either."

The two women chuckle through flowing tears.

"I love you Ky. Whatever you need, I'm here."

"Love you too, Meke."

# Chapter Fifteen

## "I'm not crazy!"

As Kyla drives to her Aunt Celeste's, Jameca's words ring through her mind, drowning out the music on the radio. She knew there was some level of peer rivalry where her and Jameca were concerned, but she had no idea to what extent until now. But right now, she's more concerned with her disappearing scar.

Kyla knows that Jameca would not be able to understand, so she decides a special trip to Celeste's is much needed. She looks at the journal lying on the seat and tries to rehearse exactly how she will explain what has happened. But, the more she rehearses, the more ridiculous she it sounds, even to herself. Then, she thinks about how grateful she is to have her aunt.

Celeste has reached out to family and helped to solidify Caleb's funeral arrangements. Her assistance is making this trying time just a little easier for Kyla.

Now nervous about trying to explain an unexplainable phenomenon, Kyla has reached her destination. She sits in her car and watches the front door before exiting her vehicle. Once she approaches the door, Kyla stands there without knocking. As if she possesses some psychic connection with Kyla, Celeste opens the front door as if anticipating her arrival.

"Aunt Ce Ce!" Kyla is startled.

"C'mon in here child. What you doin' jus' standin' out here?"

"I was just about to knock."

Or run back to my car, she thought.

"I just got back from taking one of those Uber things to go see your father. So, how are you feeling?" Aunt Ce Ce asks her as she escorts Kyla to their favorite spot on the couch.

"Okay, I guess. How's he doing?"

"Still not awake." Celeste said somberly.

"Can I ask you something?"

"Of course, anything."

"Do you remember the scar that I had right here? I got it in a fight when I was sixteen." Kyla says, pointing to her hairline.

"No, I can't say that I do."

Kyla sighs deeply. "Neither did Jameca."

"I don't understand. Why are you searching for a scar that isn't there? Are you okay, child?" Celeste places her hand on Kyla's forehead.

"I'm fine. At least I think I am anyway."

"Speak, Gal!" Celeste insists.

Kyla pulls out her old journal, with the note still jotted in the top left corner of the page. She explains about how the support group suggests journaling as a coping strategy and the events from the night before. But when she begins to read the events from her childhood journal to Celeste, the story is completely different.

"No! Wait! This isn't what I read last night. This isn't what happened. I mean it did, but it didn't. Okay, this is impossible. Why would I leave this note to myself, not to do something, that I never did?! This isn't making any sense!"

"Calm down, child."

"But Aunt Ce Ce, I'm not crazy! You have to believe me!"

"Well, I've known you for a good while now, and there has been nothing that tells me you're crazy. Now calm down. Has it ever occurred to you that there may be other forces at work here?"

"Other forces? What is that supposed to mean?" Kyla asks with skepticism.

Celeste looks at Kyla seriously. "In my years, I have witnessed many things that were meant for me and no one else. Things that if I did not see them with my own eyes, I wouldn't have believed them myself. So, at this point in my life, I know that many things are possible. Kyla, the spirit world is very different from this world we live in. The rules are different. It is when you are able to transcend the rules from the spirit world, into your own, that you begin to experience miracles and wonders."

"Tee Tee, I don't understand any of that." Kyla becomes visibly and emotionally frustrated and is on the verge of tears.

"Sweetheart." Celeste's voice begins to soothe her as she gently touches Kyla's cheek. "Somewhere along this journey you've began to surrender. Your spirit is starting to understand that surrender is not about weakness, it is about the strength to trust and give in to something much greater than yourself. Surrender to your faith. But first, you must find it. To trust in God, is to know that His Will for your life is the only Will."

Kyla is utterly confused and completely defeated by what Celeste is telling her.

"But what about the scar. . .the journal? What am I supposed to do?"

"Mon Coeur, I don't know the rules to this mystical thing you seem to be experiencing. But, in my experience with spiritual matters, nothing good comes from dishonesty. So, whatever you are dealing with, use integrity, and truth. And do not reveal the future. It sounds like your choices must be made with wisdom. And most important, seek God for the answers you seek."

"So, you believe me?!" Kyla's eyes light up.

"As I said, I know that many things are possible, and we never know from what situation the energy and will power to make the impossible happen may come from. So, I say, have faith child, and learn the lesson God is trying to teach you. If this process of coping is opening access to your spirit man, then you go with it."

Kyla isn't sure how she feels about her aunt's response to her experience, but she's relieved to not be dismissed completely. She feels she is being led on a journey, to where she's not sure, and to accomplish what she has no idea. Right now, she is as confused as she has ever been about anything, and all she wants is clarity. But will clarity come when it's too late to apply it to her life?

"Tee Tee, why do you seem to know more about this than you're saying?"

"Wisdom can be a scary thing. Sometimes we know, even when we don't realize we know." Celeste says, communicating more with her eyes than her words.

"Why does everything always seem like a riddle when you explain it?"

"Because life is just one big riddle. But trust me, you will find the answers, Mon Coeur. Just keep living."

"I'm trying to Tee Tee. I'm definitely trying."

# Chapter Sixteen

## *"I am not that chick."*

Exhausted from her day of big reveals, Kyla
winds down for the evening in anticipation of visiting
The Kingdom House the next morning. Being faced
with her own mortality and the strange events
surrounding her, she feels that opening herself up to
the possibility of something greater than herself can't
hurt her circumstances any more that they already
have been. And as much as she attempts to push
Caleb's death and her father's illness to the back of her
mind, she's still on a silent countdown to the day Caleb
is put to rest, without her father's knowledge. The
thought alone makes her feel a sickness in her
stomach. But, the thought of seeing Donovan at
church, redirects that feeling and is replace by joyful

anticipation. Right on cue, Kyla's thoughts are interrupted by Arron's now nightly call to her phone.

She doesn't recognize the number, but she knows it's him. This will be the fourth unidentified number she has had to block since being tricked by an unknown number the night before. She wishes he was as persistent about being a good man. As curious as she is about what he could possibly have to say, she realizes that whatever it is, it is likely be counterproductive to her process of moving on with the life she has left.

Thoughts of Donovan and Arron, give her very different feelings, which lead to very different memories from her journals.


*I wish I would have stood up for Donovan today. . .*

*Twenty-two years ago – Kyla age fourteen*

*At public high school in St. Louis, being popular and well-known almost certainly guaranteed that you would be treated like a super-star, and Kyla had it all.*

*She was smart, attractive, well-dressed, a talented singer, and happened to be best-friends with the most popular girl in school, Jameca Wilborn. Although, being popular granted her exceptional treatment, it was no indication of how she treated others.*

*As Kyla, Jameca, and a few more girls in their clique made their way through the crowded hallway, the girls' reaction to their peers were full of judgment. They got their jollies ridiculing and making fun of those they deemed inferior to them in any way.*

*"Girl, do you see those shoes Jabari got on? Buddies!" Jameca said, as she poked fun at a classmate that walked down the hallway.*

*Kyla felt the need to prove she could be just as cruel, and decided to join in.*

*"And look at this bitch hair! Thirsty much?"*

*All five girls erupted into laughter.*

*And then it happened. Kyla spotted Donovan in the distance, walking in their direction. He wasn't popular. He didn't wear designer clothing. And despite the fact that he was cute, Jameca didn't approve of his* height. So, every chance she got, she made fun of him and she expected Kyla to chime in. Up until that point, Kyla had been able to avoid being mean to him. She shared a class with him and they often talked and laughed with one another. But, in her need for acceptance by the "in crowd", she wouldn't be caught dead talking to him outside of class, and definitely not in Jameca's presence.

"Oh snap! Here comes the inch-high private eye!" Jameca said, referring to Donovan's height, trench coat, and glasses.

Not yet in ear shot of the jeering, Donovan flashed Kyla a smile, but she quickly turned her head and ignored his gesture as if she never saw him. But it was obvious to him that she did.

"Whatchu lookin' at, Webster?" Jameca said, when she noticed his focus was on Kyla.

The girls' outburst of laughter caused him to hang his head as he continued past them and on to his next class.

"I think somebody's got a crush on you." Jameca joked.

*"Whatever." Kyla said, trying to cover up her mutual emotions for Donovan.*

*Guilt-ridden and embarrassed by her own actions, Kyla glanced back at him as he walked away. She was empathetic to his plight and felt embarrassed as if she herself were the butt of Jameca's jokes.*

While remembering how mean she had been to the nicest boy she had ever met, she thinks about Arron and how he had never been deserving of the loyalty and compassion he has been privy to with her. She wonders how she can be so nice to someone as arrogant and disloyal as Arron. So, against her better judgment, she looks for the journal entry from the day she met him, in an effort to remember why she gave him the time of day in the first place.

*Today I met the most beautiful man I've ever seen . .*

*Five years ago – Kyla age thirty-one*

Kyla had just made partner at her investment firm and she was ready to celebrate with her friends. Jameca, planned a girls' night out to commemorate Kyla's promotion. Kyla, Jameca, and two of Kyla's friends from college, Nola and Jordin, set out in a stretch Mercedes SUV to hit as many of the city's hot spots as they could, in the time they had the limousine.

As they headed for the third club of the evening, all four women were filled with wine and spirits, and they were all ready to keep the party going.

"Where to next ladies?" The driver asked.

Just then, a classic Bob Marley song began to blast through the speakers, and Kyla instantly began to roll her hips in her seat.

"Aw yeah! I want to get down to some island music, mon!" Kyla said, in her best Jamaican accent. "Take us to a reggae club."

"I'm down with that. Jordin, hand me that bottle of rum so I can get in a Jamaican mood!" An already inebriated Jameca demanded.

They all took shots of rum and celebrated the anticipation of their next destination. The venue was obvious as they pulled in front of the building that brandished a Jamaican flag above the doorway. The chauffeur opened the door for the ladies to exit the vehicle, and they filed out one-by-one, with the next even more attractive than the one before. In fact, all four ladies were stunning their own rite. Men that approached the club, watched in amazement as the four exotic beauties exited the limo and made their way inside.

The music could be felt before it could be heard. Upon entrance to the club, Kyla was immediately caught up in the atmosphere and the music. She floated on melodic air as she made her way to the dancefloor alone. Her hips bounced to the off-beat reggae rhythm, while her small waist rotated to the staccato beats of percussion instruments.

Most of the men watched with lustful eyes at the sexy, enchanting woman with the confident and carefree aura. But of those watching, only one caught Kyla's attention. As the two made obvious eye contact, the man slowly made his way to the floor to be the only man brave enough to approach the woman every man and even a few women had been watching. They danced sensuously as only one can to reggae music for the next three songs without speaking one verbal word to one another. But the unspoken communication spoke volumes.

And then suddenly, after the end of the third song, Kyla left the dancefloor and returned to her friends who already had a drink waiting for her.

"Thank you, girl." Kyla said, as Nola handed her a Long Island Tea.

"Girl, that fine ass man you were dancing with won't take his eyes off you." Nola said, as she watched him watching Kyla.

"He is fine, isn't he? But he'll have to come to me. I'm sure a man that looks like that is used to being chased. And I am not that chick." Kyla rolled her eyes.

But, before she had the chance to continue, the man was standing in front of her with his hand stretched in her direction.

"Hello, I'm Arron. What name could a woman as beautiful as you possibly possess?"

All four women looked at each other, dazzled by his approach.

Jameca leaned over and whispered to Jordin. "Damn, he's got game."

Kyla placed her hand in his and to her surprise, instead of a handshake he raised her hand to his lips where he placed a gentle, lingering kiss, accompanied by piercing eye contact.

"Ky." Kyla said softly, mesmerized by his charm.

He reached into his pocket and handed Kyla a business card.

"Please call me." He said as he continued to look deeply into her eyes.

His presence calmed her and made her nervous at the same time. No stranger had ever made her feel that way before. Truthfully, no man had ever made her feel that way before.

"I'll think about it." Kyla smiled as she took the card.

Arron stopped a waitress as she walked by the ladies table. "The next round of drinks for these ladies is on me." Then he turned back to the table. "You ladies have a beautiful evening."


Kyla now remembers what intrigued her about him in the first place.

"I can't believe I fell for that for five years." She says aloud.

She writes a second note in the top left corner of the page, now to her 31-year-old self.

Ky,

Walk away from the charming guy at the reggae club. Charm is not all it's cracked up to be. TRUST ME!

Signed,

Yourself

# Chapter Seventeen

## "It's nice to meet you too."

Sunday morning is usually Kyla's day to get some much-needed rest, but not today. She is determined to expose herself to a deeper existence. Not to mention, she is hoping to run into Donovan at church today. Ignoring the pain that sent her to Dr. Okai's office two weeks ago, Kyla lights a cigarette as she gets dolled up for church. She even does her ritualistic facial inventory without a thought about the missing scar. The rest of her morning routine goes on as usual, and she darts out of the door on her way to The Kingdom House.

Within a block of church, she checks the mirror to be sure that her face doesn't yet reflect her diagnoses. Once she arrives, she takes a few deep breaths to calm the butterflies in her stomach. Although, anxious to open herself up to something new, church makes Kyla unexplainably nervous. But she powers through and walks through the doors with purpose. With her head held high she walks to a pew midway between the first and the last and sits in a seat closes to the isle. Kyla feels accomplished as she pulls out a notebook to jot down notes from the anticipated sermon.

Just then, Kyla feels a hand on her shoulder.

"Kyla, I'm glad you decided to come back!"

She immediately recognizes the voice as Donovan's, and she stands to greet him with a hug. But as she turns to lean in, Kyla notices the very attractive, caramel colored woman standing next to him.

"I wanted to introduce you to my wife, Skye. Skye, this is Kyla, the woman I told you about."

Kyla, now wondering what he could have possibly told his wife about her, stands there and pretends she doesn't feel the sting of unwarranted jealousy penetrating through her.

125

Skye reaches out and wraps her arms around Kyla. "Oh, welcome sister! It's so good to have you."

"Oh, thank you." Kyla says trying to catch up to Skye's abrupt interruption of her personal space. "It's nice to meet you too."

Kyla is caught completely off guard and is feeling awkward in this situation.

"Well, I guess I'll see you later." Kyla says unexpectedly as she turns to sit back down.

Donovan and Skye look at one another with indifference and decides it's best to give her some space.

"Okay well, it was good to see you again." Donovan says, unsure if he should say anything.

As he walks away, he turns to see Kyla shaking her head in her hands and hopes she is alright.

"A wife. I should've known he was married." Kyla says under her breath.

Now she feels convicted about her excitement to come to church more to see Donovan than to hear

God's Word. She knows she should really be focused on the matter at hand, her life; not Donovan. Service is starting, and she knows it's too late to move to the back row of the church. So, as much as she wants to retreat into solitude, she stays put as the pastor approaches the pulpit.

"Good morning, children of God!" The pastor bellows. "I am so excited about today's message!"

The pastor picks up a small orange devotional and flips through the pages.

"I woke up this morning and read a passage from this daily devotional by Sarah Young, called Jesus Calling, that set my soul on fire! 'I am with you and for you. You face nothing alone – nothing! When you feel anxious, know that you are focusing on the visible world and leaving me out of the picture. The remedy is simple: Fix your eyes not on what is seen, but what is unseen. Verbalize your trust in Me, the Living One who sees you always. I will get you safely through this day and all your days. But you can find Me only in the present. Each day is a precious gift from My Father. How ridiculous to grasp for future gifts when today's is set before you! Receive today's gifts gratefully, unwrapping it tenderly and delving into its depths. As you savor this gift, you find me.'

As I read this, my spirit began to grieve for those that need to hit rock bottom before they recognize or even search for the power of God the Father, our Creator. But the reality is, in our weakness, God's strength is magnified, and I began to rejoice for them. 2 Corinthians 4:17-18 says, 'For our light and momentary troubles are achieving for us an eternal glory that far outweighs them all. So, we fix our eyes not on what is seen, but on what is unseen, since what is seen is temporary, but what is unseen is eternal.' This tells me that our heavenly God, the unseen, is greater that our very clearly seen earthly troubles. Which is why our earthly troubles belong in the hands of a heavenly power that can change any circumstances, no matter what it looks like! Isaiah 40:31 tells us that, 'they that wait upon the Lord shall renew their strength; they shall mount up with wings as eagles; they shall run, and not be weary; and they shall walk, and not faint.' Did you know that God waits for you to call on and trust Him so that He can prove to the world through you, that He is alive and operating in our lives? Well, He does. He is. He's waiting to show you who's God! He's waiting to show the world miracles through your life! He is capable of changing every aspect of your life!"

The sermon, that seems to be only for her, leaves Kyla emotional and teary eyed. She sits long after service is over. Church goers fellowship around her, but recollection of the pastor's words about faith and miracles drown out the surrounding atmosphere. She wonders if she is deserving of a miracle as her memory is flooded with moments that make her ashamed of herself. The grudge she holds against her father. Her mistreatment of Caleb and Donovan. The untold secrets. Kyla is afraid that if she thinks hard enough, she will only dredge up more disappointment.

She wipes her face and gathers her belongings. On her way to her vehicle she sees Donovan and Skye in the distance. In her disappointment, she hadn't noticed before that Skye is pregnant. She appears five or six months along, and the care that Donovan takes with her rivals any knight in shining armor. He looks at Skye like she is the only woman in the world, and Kyla only wishes she had someone that cherishes her that way. In fact, she isn't sure if she ever has.

The silent ride home is a perfect personification of the loneliness and emptiness she feels inside. Then she thinks about how selfish it is of her to expect to develop a relationship with anyone when she has no idea of her own life expectancy. What was she expecting from Donovan anyway? She begins to question her unrealistic expectations for the rest of her life and realizes it may be inexorable that she will be alone for the rest of her life.

Her whole life, she has craved the acceptance and approval of others. Even allowing people to determine who she is and how she treats others. Or deciding that who she is and what she's worth, is based on what certain people think. This morning is a reality check. She realizes that she has spent her life trying to please everyone except the One that has accepted her all along, her heavenly Father.

# Chapter Eighteen

## "I must be losing my mind."

With one day until Caleb's funeral, Kyla wants to be sure everyone has been contacted and all the arrangements are set. And thanks to her Aunt Celeste everything seems to be in order. It has also been a few days since she went to visit Theo. It makes her distraught to see her father helpless and unconscious, which only reminds her that he is still unaware of his only son's death. So, she has avoided the thought of visiting altogether. However, she is sure to call and check on him daily.

Kyla decides to take a month's leave from work. Her company is still unaware of her diagnosis, so she takes a stress leave that to their knowledge is due to her brother's death and her father's illness. But today, she is up early so that she can visit Dr. Okai's office for further test results and a treatment plan. Nonetheless, her morning will not start without her coffee. She checks the cupboard and to her dismay she is out of dark roast. Without hesitation, Kyla throws on a Tee-shirt, joggers, and flip flops and heads to the grocery store. On her way out of the door she checks her phone and to her relief there are no strange numbers in her call log.

As she casually strolls down the coffee isle making life decisions about what coffee will do the trick, Kyla hears a chillingly familiar voice.

"I thought I saw you come down this row."

She frantically looks around for somewhere to hide, but it's too late. There stands Arron at the end of the row looking in her direction.

"Babe, I've been looking all over for you." He says.

Kyla, let's her guard down and prepares to defend her stance once again on their break up. But before she can even part her lips, a woman's voice coming from behind her, stops Kyla in her tracks.

"I told you I needed coffee." The attractive woman that appears to be mixed with something other than Black says, before looking down at the adorable little replica of Arron holding her hand. "And AJ here was going to just die if he didn't get some hot chocolate."

"Daddy look!" The excited little boy holding a box of hot chocolate, who looks to be about four years old, says to Arron.

Kyla stands in shock as Arron walks past her with no acknowledgement whatsoever. She is outraged and embarrassed that he is acting like he doesn't even know who she is. She watches as Arron goes over and picks up the little boy and kisses him on the cheek, before grabbing the hand of the woman who appears to be wearing a wedding ring that matches the ring he is wearing.

The family walks together to the end of the isle when Arron stops suddenly and turns to address Kyla. "Excuse me, but is your name Ky?" Arron asks Kyla.

133

"What?" Is the only thing Kyla can manage to say.

"Really Babe? Is this her?" Arron's attractive companion joins in.

The couple, with the toddler in tow, heads back in Kyla's direction. Arron reaches down and grabs Kyla's hand to shake it.

"I'm sorry, my name is Arron. You probably don't remember me, but we met at a reggae club about five years ago. And, I know this may seem strange, but I said I would never forget you and I would let you know if I ever saw you again that that night changed my life. You changed my life." He chuckles before continuing. "I never thought I would do this, but I thank you for rejecting me. It was a wake-up call that was a pivotal moment in my life."

"I guess I should thank you too." The woman interjects while looking lovingly into Arron's eyes. "We met that night. He was so upset, that he left the club early. He called an UBER, I showed up, and the rest is history." She says kissing the little boy on the cheek.

134

"Um." Kyla says, as she stands there dumbfounded.

The couple looks at one another, and Arron addresses Kyla once more. "Well, we didn't mean to bother you. I just wanted to say thanks."

They walk away leaving Kyla with no words. She forgets to grab her coffee and she hurriedly makes her way to her car. Once inside, she grabs the steering wheel and attempts to slow her breathing to prevent a full-on panic attack.

Kyla drives home without remembering a stop sign, stop light, or a turn in either direction. She is literally on automatic pilot as the scene in the grocery store plays over and over in her mind. By the time she makes it home, she is insistent upon rereading the entry in her journal of the night she met Arron. But this act only causes further trepidation when she flips through the pages of the journal and reveals that the night happened exactly as Arron described. Just then, a barrage of unfamiliar memories begins to push the five-year relationship that she remembers so vividly, into a distant recollection. Finally, she runs to her jewelry box where she retired the promise ring Arron had given her. But after savagely searching, she found nothing.

"This can't be possible. I must be losing my mind."

She immediately calls Jameca. The phone rings four or five times before she answers.

"Hey lady, what's up?" Jameca answers.

"So, I saw Arron today with another woman, that looked like she could be his wife, and their baby! That son of a bitch tried to act like he didn't even know me!" Kyla rants.

"Arron? Who is Arron?"

"You know, the loser?" Kyla tries to juggle Jameca's memory by using her own nickname for Arron.

"Is that the guy you went out with a few weeks ago?"

"Never mind. I'll call you back." Kyla says and then hangs up the phone.

Jameca calls right back, but Kyla powers her phone off. The room is closing in around her and she feels like a character in an episode of the Twilight Zone. She is now as alert as any amount of caffeine will make her when her alarm sounds to remind her of her doctor's appointment. Discombobulated and confused, she heads to the doctor's office hoping that maybe what she hears from the doctor will shed some light on her recent unexplained experiences. At this point, Kyla is not sure whether or not she is hallucinating or if something mystical is afoot, but she is overly determined to find out what is happening in her head.

# Chapter Nineteen

## "But I feel fine!"

Kyla is still in a daze when she enters the doctor's office waiting room. She replays "Mr. and Mrs. Arron Johnson's" gratitude in her mind, while she has to concentrate very hard to recall moments in her and Arron's relationship. She is beginning to wonder if there was ever a relationship to begin with. Then she starts to recall seeing Arron in passing and has to ponder whether she has imagined it all. She is so into her own thoughts; Kyla doesn't hear the nurse calling her name until the third time she is called.

"Kyla LaRue!"

"Oh, I'm sorry. Yes, I'm here."

The nurse leads Kyla to an examination room at the end of the hallway.

"Dr. Okai will be right with you."

Kyla leans on the edge of the exam table with her purse resting on her knees. Her head is clouded, and she can't seem to focus. So many things are running through her mind, yet she can't concentrate on a single thought.

Dr. Okai enters the room after knocking several times, with no answer. She examines Kyla's thoughtless expression with focus-less eyes and partially parted lips. Kyla has not even noticed the doctor's entrance.

Dr. Okai snaps her fingers in front of Kyla's eyes. "Ms. LaRue?"

Kyla snaps out of her dazed state and looks around the exam room as if unaware of her surroundings momentarily.

"Oh, I'm sorry doctor. Did you say something?"

The doctor sits on the stool in front of Kyla and pulls out a small flash light.

"Can you follow this light with your eyes for me?"

Kyla does as the doctor requests.

"Are you experiencing any headaches, dizziness, loss of time, confusion, or hallucinations?" The doctor asks.

"Why? What's going on?" Kyla asks.

Dr. Okai puts the flashlight back into her pocket and places her arms across her chest.

"It appears that the Cancer has spread to your brain. And because your Cancer is in its advanced stages, it's hard to determine how quickly it's spreading. It's important that you be cognizant of your mental deterioration. Have you blacked out or had any seizures that you know of?" The doctor asks seriously.

"No. No, I haven't blacked out or had any seizures. I mean, some really strange things have been happening, but. . . Cancer in my brain?"

It is as if saying it aloud makes it register somehow. Now, she questions her own judgement on everything that's happened.

140

"So, what does this mean? Does this change my life expectancy?"

Dr. Okai looks down at her shoes and takes a deep breath.

"It is very difficult to tell you assuredly, but with treatment you have roughly 90 days. As a matter of fact, you may want to consider getting a driver and a caregiver." The doctor admits.

"But I feel fine!"

"That's right. You feel fine, until you don't. Then it will be too late to tell your loved ones what you want and need. It's better to be proactive in situations like this. And also, if you haven't already, you should really stop smoking and drinking if you want to preserve what life you have left."

"So, how long without treatment?" Kyla dares to ask.

"Weeks. To be honest, Ms. LaRue, I'm surprised you are still getting around so well. Based on the progression of the disease, you could be debilitated any day now."

141

Kyla doesn't want to share her experiences with her doctor for fear that it will only confirm Dr. Okai's diagnoses. A whirlwind of questions began to circle her psyche: Has her perceived reality only been a Cancer induced figment of her imagination? Has what she remembers about her own life simply been hallucinations? Or has the seemingly, absolutely impossible events that have taken place been an actuality? And most pressing, has her secret prayers and silent faith contributed to the impossible? Aside from being confused, Kyla is devasted by the new developments in her illness.

She sits silently on the edge of the exam table, looking in the doctor's direction. But Kyla doesn't see the doctor, nor does she see anything else in the room. Her eyes focus on nothing as she tries to figure out what she can accomplish in just a few months.

Dr. Okai decides to interrupt the uncomfortable silence. "Ms. LaRue, we can start your radiation this week, if you'd like?"

As though she has been shocked with an electric charge, Kyla jumps up from the table and bolts out the door. She can hear Dr. Okai's voice call her name in the distance as she leaves the suite and heads straight to her car.

Once secure in the privacy of her vehicle, Kyla belts the loudest scream she has ever produced. "Ahhhhhhhh!!!!"

She screams as long as her breath will allow. And then she is dead silent, sitting still, staring into the windshield at nothing. A feeling of helpless hopelessness washes over her and all she feels is defeat. Defeated by love, defeated by life, and now she will be defeated by death before she's ready. Although, she doesn't want to utter one word, Kyla knows she needs to talk to someone. So, she looks at her screensaver and calls the number on the flyer hoping to reach Heaven.

The phone begins to ring, and she contemplates hanging up, but then there is voice on the other end.

"Um, hello? May I please speak with Heaven?"

"This is she." Heaven's chipper voice almost lightens the moment.

143

"Hi Heaven. This is Kyla. I hope it's okay that I called." Her voice reveals more than her words.

"It's absolutely fine! Is everything okay?"

Kyla pauses for a moment before answering. Heaven can now feel the tension through the phone line.

"Kyla?"

"My doctor just told me that the Cancer has spread to my brain. . . I don't. . . I'm not ready to die!"

Kyla exposes her raw emotions to Heaven, becoming choked up as she attempts to speak.

"Oh, heavenly Father!" Heaven reacts to the news.

"I'm sorry. I just didn't know who else to call. Can I ask you something?"

"Sure."

"When you were diagnosed, did you experience any hallucinations or remembering things differently than they actually happened?" Kyla asks, searching for some understanding.

144

"Well, not exactly. First, the headaches started, and then I started to forget things. But at my worst, my speech and balance were affected terribly."

Kyla looks at her reflection in the rearview mirror and fights to hold back the tears filling her eyes. She is desperate; desperate to live through a deadly diagnosis, desperate to find answers to the discrepancies between her memories and her actual experiences, and she is most desperate to know if miracles are real.

"How did you come back from it?"

"Kyla, all I did was pray and have unmovable faith. I spoke healing all the time, no matter how I felt. I thanked God for healing that my body had not yet experienced. But most important, I accepted God's Will for my life, no matter what it was; life or death. I understand that my purpose reaches far beyond this existence. This earth experience or grooming process, as I call it, is only a prelude to what we are destined for in this universe. I know I'm probably going a little over your head with all of this, but you want to know how I overcame it, and this was my process. I have to believe it helped me. Have you prayed?"

"I talk to God from time to time, if that's what you mean?

"No, I mean really prayed. Confess and profess from the depths of your soul, to Him? Don't you know that you can't hide anything from Him, so what are you holding back? He's waiting for you to trust Him."

Kyla sits quietly with the phone in her hand.

"I don't know." She finally answers.

"It's about choice, really. The choices we make determine the path for our lives. Allow your choices to be led by God. Choose to go to Him with transparency, about everything."

"You make having faith sound so easy."

"No, it isn't easy. But it is necessary."

"Well, I don't want to take up any more of your time. Thank you for listening, and for sharing." Kyla says with sincerity.

"Anytime. Can I pray with you before you go?" Heaven offers.

"Sure." Kyla says, sounding very unsure.

Kyla closes her eyes and allows Heaven to cry out to God on her behalf. Silent tears roll down her face, finding their home on the front of her blouse. For the first time, Kyla listens with her heart while Heaven prays. She realizes that now is the time for her to trust something outside of herself, to trust in the "impossible".

After the meaningful conversation with Heaven, Kyla goes straight home and pulls out her chest filled with journals. She remembers everything that Heaven tells her, but what seems to ring the loudest is what she said about choices determining the path for our lives. Now resolute on finding out what decisions have brought her to this place, Kyla decides to start with her very first journal entry, twenty-two years ago on her fourteenth birthday; before her life began to turn upside down.

# Chapter Twenty

## *"Boo!"*

*My first birthday wish is to send Caleb back to where he came from. . .*

*Twenty-Two Years Ago – Kyla's Fourteenth Birthday*

Kyla was awakened by a stiff blow to the face with a pillow which caused her to open her eyes to her daily calendar displaying 'my 14th birthday' written across the date, March 22nd.

"Happy birthday! That's one!" Nine-year-old Caleb screamed before he smacked Kyla again. "Two!"

She held up her hands to avoid a third blow to the face.

"Get out you little ingrate!"

"What? I'm just giving you your birthday licks." Caleb said with a dubious grin.

"I hate you, you little fucker!" Kyla said through clenched teeth.

"I'm telling Ma, you cussin'."

Kyla struggled to sift through the covers so that she could get to Caleb. But he knew what would happen if she got loose before he vacated the premises, so he made a mad dash for his bedroom.

"Mom!" Caleb screamed on his way down the hallway.

"He's lying Mom!" Kyla retorted.

"Stop that nonsense and come down for breakfast; both of you! Shilynne commanded.

Kyla already had her birthday outfit pressed, laid out, and ready to go. She quickly dressed and made her way downstairs to the kitchen. On her way down the steps, she could smell pancakes and a plethora of breakfast meats, and she could hear her mother's and Caleb's voice. She was pleasantly surprised when she entered to find her mother had made her famous birthday cakes: Pancakes, topped with whipped cream, strawberries, and chocolate syrup; Kyla's favorite.

"Happy birthday, beautiful!" Shilynne belted.

It was always like the sun had just parted the clouds when entering a room with Shilynne. She was a bright light during the darkest times.

"Where's daddy?" Kyla asked, irritated by her father's constant absence as of late.

"He wanted to keep his food down today. He said he wanted to leave before you came down, so he didn't have to see your face." Caleb made his crack at Kyla.

"Shut up, brat!"

"It's too early for that! And I don't want to hear it! Now, to answer your question, your father had an early meeting. But he told me to give you this."

Shilynne handed Kyla a card-sized envelope.

Kyla smiled from ear-to-ear as she ripped open the envelope to reveal a birthday card containing $50 and a personal hand-written note.

*I'm sorry I couldn't see you this morning, but you know I love you baby girl. Enjoy your day! Love Daddy.*

"Why does daddy have so many early meetings lately?" Kyla inquired.

"I don't know. Business is picking up, I guess."

Shilynne turned toward the stove and continued to place food on the table. Kyla watched as her mother tirelessly prepared the breakfast table that she knew full well her mother expected her father to be there to enjoy. Kyla wasn't buying her mother's nonchalant attitude about Theo's absence. But, Shilynne had the ultimate Poker face.

"You look really pretty today, birthday girl!"

"Thanks Mom." Kyla smiled.

"LIES."

*"Caleb, you are one more comment away from a sore butt."* Shilynne threatened.

*He was clearly annoyed by his childish display of pouting and mumbling under his breath. Kyla however, couldn't be happier to see him being scolded. So much so, that she continued to antagonize Caleb by stealing food from his plate, knowing he would protest out loud, while on his last leg with Shilynne. What she didn't expect was the swift kick to the shin she received from Caleb. Stifling her wince of pain, Kyla reached under the table and pinched Caleb's thigh as hard as she could.*

*"Ow!" Caleb Screamed.*

*"What now?!" Shilynne said with abrupt aggravation.*

*"Kyla. . ."*

*"Caleb, I don't want to hear it! You're done! Get up from the table and go to the bus stop. I'm tired of your mess!"*

*"But. . ."*

"But, nothing. I've had enough! Goodbye. Have a good day." Shilynne said with her finger pointed out the door.

Kyla gave Caleb a devious smirk as he forcefully pushed through the screen door without finishing his breakfast. Caleb was so angry; a single tear escaped his eye as he walked outside with a scowl on his face.

"And you," Shilynne interrupted Kyla's silent antagonism, "you're the oldest. I really need you to do better with being an example and stop stooping to his level. All you two will have is each other one day."

"Yes ma'am." Kyla said, looking down into her plate. "I'm sorry."

Shilynne looked at her growing baby girl with endearing eyes, before she kissed her on the forehead to ease the obvious guilt etched across her face.

"I love you, sweetheart. Enjoy your day."

"I love you too, Mom."

Kyla finished her birthday breakfast and proceeded to meet her friends. As she approached the

153

corner where she met Jameca and her crew every morning, she could see four mylar balloons, one held by each girl, bouncing in her direction. All four girls wore an identical dress to Kyla's, all in different colors.

"Happy birthday, beeeach!" Jameca screamed from yards away.

All four girls excitedly ran in Kyla's direction and bombarded her with hugs and balloons.

"Aw, thank yawl!"

"Girl, you know birthdays are special, especially if you're one of my girls!" Jameca exclaimed.

The five fashionable and fit, fabulous teenage girls made their way to the bus stop. Kyla, with four balloons in tow, felt like the most important person in the world that day. She couldn't wait to get to school so that she could be the center of attention all day long.

While on the bus, the group of girls indulged in mindless chatter, oblivious to the boys around them gawking as if sharing a bus ride with celebrities. They were usually so wrapped up in themselves, they rarely noticed others without intention.

"So, Ky, what did your dad say about letting you have a birthday / spring break party?" Jameca asked.

"He didn't say anything. I haven't seen him in almost two weeks. My mom says he has all these early and late meetings. So, I haven't even thought about it." Her voice had a tinge of disappointment. "Besides, I am not trying to spend anymore time with Travis than necessary."

Kyla had agreed to go to the spring dance with Travis, only because Jameca wanted to go with his best friend Derek. Kyla saw nothing attractive about Travis, from his appearance to his personality.

"How could you not think about celebrating your birthday?" Jameca was taken aback.

"It's cool. I'll settle for the school spring dance." Kyla said sarcastically.

"You suck!" Jameca expressed as the bus approached the school.

Even with all of the excitement surrounding her birthday, the only thing Kyla could think about was seeing Donovan. During her first year of high school, *seeing him had actually become the highlight of her day, along with choir class. Not wanting ridicule from her popular clique of friends, Kyla thought up an excuse to part ways with them, so she could walk to class with Donovan.*

*"I gotta see the counselor before class. I'll catch up with yawl before 2nd period." She lied.*

*Kyla hurriedly turned in the opposite direction and made a beeline for Donovan's locker. Just as she'd hoped, there he stood, gathering his books for his next two classes. She slowly made her way next to his locker and stood on the other side of his open locker door, hiding her balloons behind her back.*

*"Boo!" Kyla startled Donovan as he closed the locker door.*

*Clearly surprised, he dropped his English book along with a thin gift-wrapped package. Kyla could tell that he was made nervous by her presence and embarrassed by his own nervousness. Kyla and Donovan both bent down to pick up his belongings. They reached for the English book at the same time and their fingers lightly touched, but the lingering eye*

156

contact seemed to last forever, until Donovan abruptly ended the moment and quickly moved his hand from the book and onto the package.

"Um, this is for you. Happy Birthday."

"You got me a birthday gift?" She asked with delighted confusion.

"I hope that's okay."

"Of course, it is! I just didn't expect it, that's all. Thank you!"

She excitedly rushed to open the package to reveal a pastel colored journal with sunflowers on the cover, that read 'I hope your day shines as bright as you do'.

"This is so cute! Sunflowers are my favorite!" She squealed.

"I know. I remembered from your introduction in class last year. Let's see, sunflowers, weeping willows, and sea green. Favorite flower, tree, and color, right?"

She was impressed. But even more, she was completely infatuated with Donovan. Despite her friends, she liked him and there was nothing she could do about it. She thought about him all the time, while imagining he was popular, and they were girlfriend and boyfriend. He was cute, and thoughtful, and nice, and smart. . . everything that mattered to her. But it would not be enough for Jameca and the crew. She wished she had the courage to not care what they thought.

Donovan noticed Kyla flip through the empty pages when she got to her seat.

"It's a journal. You know, like a best-friend that can't tell all your secrets to anyone." He told her.

"I like that idea. Do you have one?"

"Naw, but my twin does. She writes in it every day."

"Thanks again." She said, before sticking the notebook in her bookbag.

"Are you going to the dance?" Donovan caught her off guard with the question.

"Um, I think so. Are you?"

Her heart raced at the thought that he was about to ask her to the dance. But she was conflicted. On one hand, she was excited and flattered that he would want to go with her. But, on the other hand, she had already promised to go with Travis and she was not at all ready for the ridicule.

"Nah." He said, crushing her dreams and relieving her fears all at the same time. "That's not really my thing, especially without a date."

"I can understand that, I guess."

"Yeah, I just can't wait to grow up and marry a good woman, so I can treat her like my dad does my mom. He loves her a lot."

The more Kyla got to know about Donovan, the more she like him.

"You're ready to get married at fourteen?" Kyla chuckled.

"Of course not. But I look forward to that part of being an adult. How do your parents get along?"

"Okay, I guess. I hardly ever see my dad anymore. He works a lot."

159

"Well, no matter how much I work, I'll always find time to take my wife on dates and buy her flowers." He assured her.

"Sounds like you're gonna make some girl a really lucky woman someday."

They smile in one another's direction as the bell rang and the teacher began class.

Kyla ponders over her fourteenth birthday and the day she receives her first journal from Donovan, and what the sentiment meant to her. Without hesitation, she writes herself a note in the journal, before reading further.

*Kyla,*

*Don't be afraid to defy your friends to be nice Donovan. And be a better big sister and role model for Caleb,* love him, he may be all you have one day.

From you to yourself.

# Chapter Twenty-One

## *"I just gotta go."*

At 12:30 am, Kyla examines the old, tattered, sunflower covered journal and recalls her fourteenth birthday like it was yesterday. The journal is nostalgic and represents the time in her life when she began to realize who she really is. As she examines that time, she realizes that she never really became that person. Always so worried about the opinion of those she deems worthy of judging her, Kyla neglected to see her true identity dangling right in front of her, choosing to become the version of herself most accepted by her peers.

Jameca represents the part of her that ridicules and judge people for what they have or what they can do for her; the part of her that deep down she wishes she had never found appealing. And then, there's Donovan. He represents the part of Kyla that respects and cares for others; the part that she's suppressed for so many years. Why had she chosen to become the mean girl? As she scrutinizes her own behavior, Kyla delves further into her teenage years, deciding to dive into another journal.

*Today I wish I would have never left the house. . .*

*Twenty-One Years Ago – Kyla age fifteen*

*Every other Saturday afternoon Kyla and her girls would catch the bus to explore parts of St. Louis they had never experienced. A new mall, a new restaurant, a new recreational activity; anything unfamiliar to them would be on the agenda for the day. The new mall in Chesterfield was having its opening weekend and the girls were ready to see what the alleged Mega-mall had to offer.*

*Fashionably dressed wearing fresh hairdos, all five girls walked to the bus stop with their designer bags in tow. Jameca even had a fresh set of airbrushed acrylic nails. As Kyla admired the way Jameca maneuvered her fingers with deliberate sophistication to accentuate her nails, she knew that she would soon have to get her nails done too.*

*"You realize we're gonna have to catch like three buses one way, right?" Trena, the darkest, most curvaceous, and most attractive of the girls in Kyla's opinion, pointed out.*

*"Do you have something better to do?" Jameca snapped.*

*"Naw, I'm just saying; that's a lot of money both ways."*

*"If you don't have the money; you shouldn't have come. Don't nobody want to hear you complainin' about how much money we spendin' all day." Jameca rolled her eyes at Trena.*

*Kyla could see that Trena was clearly embarrassed by Jameca's reprimand, fueled by insecurity. So, Kyla walked up behind Trena and secretly placed a twenty-dollar bill in her hand.*

"I got you." Kyla mouthed silently to Trena.

It was times like these that made Kyla question why she wanted to be around Jameca in the first place. Then she thought about the fact that their Saturday afternoon excursions were Jameca's idea to begin with, and she remembered part of what drew her to Jameca was her ability to usher them into adventure. So, as frustrated as Kyla was with her insolence, she created enough excitement to keep Kyla intrigued.

"So, where to first?" Jameca asked, as if anyone else's opinion mattered.

"I'm hungry. Let's get something to eat first."

"Lauren, you're always hungry. I say we hit Forever 21." Jameca interjected.

Lyndsey, Lauren's twin sister was visibly irritated with Jameca's antics. She only subjected herself to Jameca because Lauren insisted on being her friend. The twins were both basketball players and freakishly tall. But despite her size, Lauren seamed completely intimidated by Jameca. Lyndsey on the other hand, felt all together differently.

"Then why did you even ask?" Lyndsey retorted, as she rolled her eyes at Jameca before stepping onto the bus.

All five girls made their way to the back of the bus, where the cat fight continued.

"I take it you have a problem with my suggestion?" Jameca asked snidely.

"It's not your suggestion I have a problem with." Lyndsey spoke at Jameca without looking in her direction, which fueled Jameca's fire.

"You got a problem with me then?" Jameca's Haitian accent could clearly be heard.

Finally, turning to face Jameca, Lyndsey stared coldly into her eyes for a few moments before she spoke.

"Jameca, I deal with you because my sister likes you, for some reason. But I promise you, THIS is not what you want."

And then, without hesitation or apprehension, Lyndsey turned her back to Jameca and continued to look out the window. Kyla had never seen Jameca

166

speechless or even back down, for that matter. Then right on cue, she tried to save face.

"Whatever, I don't have time for random drama anyway."

Jameca had a talent for starting drama, and then acting like she was above it.

"So, AFTER Forever 21, we'll go check out the food court. I hope they have a Chick-Fila." Jameca tauntingly announced.

"Well, I hope they have Sbarro's. I want pizza." Kyla joined in.

"Ooh, me too!" Trena added.

"Can you afford Sbarro's?"

"Jameca! Random drama. Remember?" Kyla said.

"I'm just sayin'"

"Cut it out, please." Kyla was almost begging.

"These bitches." Jameca whispered under her breath.

Kyla shook her head and rolled her eyes out the window. She leaned her head on the glass and hoped the rest of the day went on without incident. At that point, it was clear that Jameca was beginning to rub the others in the clique the wrong way. Kyla looked out the window as the bus prepared to make a left, and she saw a vehicle a few yards ahead that she recognized immediately; her dad's.

Waiting with excited anticipation, Kyla sat up straight in her seat hoping the bus would speed up enough for her to wave to Theo before it turned. It seemed like an eternity before she was next to her father's driver's door, waving to get his attention. And then it happened. She watched in horror as an unidentified female leaned into her father's lap and began performing oral sex on him.

Her jaw dropped, and she hadn't even realized that she had stopped breathing. Tears started to well up in her eyes and she hoped they would wash away the sight in front of her. As much as she wanted to look away, she couldn't. The disbelief and pain she felt was insurmountable.

168

*As if he could feel he was being watched, Theo looked up into the bus window, directly into Kyla's eyes. She reacted like she had been the one caught doing the unspeakable. Kyla's heart pounded as she jumped in her seat and sat facing forward with her hand blocking the side of her face.*

*"What's wrong with you?" Jameca asked, noticing a change in Kyla's demeanor.*

*"Nothing!" Kyla said snappily.*

*"Well, stop being weird."*

*Kyla frantically looked around the bus. She didn't know what to do. So, she did what was instinctive for her; she fled.*

*"I gotta go." Kyla stood and pulled the cord for the bus to stop.*

*"What? Where are you going?" Jameca asked.*

*"Yeah, what's going on?" Lyndsey chimed in.*

*"Um, nothing. I just gotta go. Yawl have fun."*

*"But. . ." was all Jameca could say before Kyla exited the back door of the bus.*

169

*Fifteen minutes later, Kyla was on a return bus home. She rode in the back with her arms folded across her chest. She was lost. She didn't know how to feel; what to think. Kyla felt that everything she thought she knew was a lie. The bus stopped a couple of blocks from her home and she reluctantly got off.*

*Hoping not to see her father, Kyla swiftly headed home as if she were on the run. She had no idea what her next actions would be. All she knew is she needed to be alone to process what she had just seen. Her mind was racing so, that she couldn't even remember how she got to the front door of her house.*

*Kyla quietly unlocked the front door and attempted to creep to her room. She was relieved that Caleb was visiting a friend and she didn't have to worry about avoiding him. There was a stale smell in the air, although familiar to her, it was something she had never smelled in her own home. She followed the scent to the dining room where she found her mother smoking a cigarette, with an almost empty bottle of Tequila in front of her on the table. The problem was, Shilynne didn't smoke or drink.*

"Mom, what are you doing?"

"I'm minding my business. What are you doing here? I thought you were gone with your friends." Shilynne slurred.

"Momma, you're drunk!"

"Ding ding ding! $500 goes to Kyla Arie LaRue! You got any other brilliant observations you wanna make?"

Kyla had never seen her mother behave in that manner.

"But you don't drink. . . or smoke." Kyla was confused.

Shilynne looked at the cigarette between her fingers and held the bottle in the air.

"Well, apparently I do." Shilynne chuckled.

Kyla on the other hand, could find nothing funny about the situation.

Shilynne attempted to stand, but her inebriation wouldn't allow her. She plopped right back down into the dining room chair, scattering cigarette ashes across

171

the dining room rug and table. Kyla ran to extinguish any sparks that threatened to materialize into fire.

"Mom! What are you doing?! Why are you acting like this?!" Kyla began to develop a knot in her throat as she fought to hold back tears of rage and confusion. "What is going on?!" She cried out.

Shilynne, unstable and emotional, staggered to the hallway on the way to her room; bottle, cigarette, and ashtray in hand. Kyla thought to herself, 'those are only for decoration', as Shilynne turned, holding the former decorative ashtray.

"Ask your father." She said, finally answering Kyla's question before exiting the room.

Kyla could see her mother's eyes fill with tears as she turned to walk away. Her heart was broken, and she couldn't imagine the pain her mother was going through. She retreated to her room and pulled out her journal; her fifth by that time. She wrote and cried for hours of the agony of betrayal coursing through her.

Kyla closes her journal and recalls that day and the days after. She remembers how her father looked at her with works unspoken. The words, 'ask you father', would often ring through her mind, but years passed, and she never did. Her relationship with her father was never the same. She now knows that she never really wanted to know the truth. Not facing it means it wasn't real in her mind.

She recalls how for months she avoids contact with her father and never speaks again to her mother about the first day she sees her smoke and drink, because it certainly wasn't her last. That day is only the first of the downward spiral that Shilynne takes until her death. Wondering now if her silence could have played a part in the demise of her family, in desperation, Kyla decides to leave another note to herself.

*Kyla,*

*Avoiding or holding in your truth can be the Cancer that spreads throughout your entire life. SPEAK*

*UP!*

*Your advice to you.*

# Chapter Twenty-Two

## *"What did I do wrong?"*

Kyla looks at her cell phone and realizes it's almost 2:00 am. Caleb's funeral is in the morning, but sleep is the last thing on her mind. She lights a cigarette and pours a shot of tequila. And then, she looks back into the chest and retrieves a black and white journal with music notes printed on the cover. She cringes slightly at the memory the journal invokes. Reluctantly, she opens the cover and relives the occurrence that was the onset of the vices she has been unable to conquer for so many years.

*I will never sing again after today. . .*

*Dr. Winston's vocal chorale class was Kyla's favorite. She loved to sing, and he loved to let her. Not to mention, her vocal class was the class right after her English class with Donovan, so she would always be in the mood to sing. But today was different, special even. Today she had to stay after school to rehearse with her favorite teacher.*

*She had been chosen to sing the solo for the chorale's next competition, and today was her first solo rehearsal with Dr. Winston. Kyla hummed her solo as she approached the choir room, where she could already hear the piano being played. Dr. Winston was an older, very slim, tall man of about six-foot-five inches and was clearly bi-racial from his appearance.*

*"There she is!" Dr. Winston announced, as Kyla entered the room.*

*"Hi Dr. Winston!"*

*"Ready to get started?" The eager vocal teacher asked.*

*"As ready as I'll ever be." Kyla sounded unsure.*

*"Ms. LaRue." The teacher looked over the top of his glasses. "I know you have the talent and potential to do this. But you must believe in yourself." He assured her.*

*"I guess I was just shocked that you picked me, a first year, to do this solo for a competition so big." Kyla admitted.*

*"Well, I have faith that you can get the job done." He smiled.*

*"Thank you, sir."*

*"Okay, let's begin!"*

*Dr. Winston began to play Kyla's part on the piano, and Kyla began to sing. He seemed pleased with her performance and creative decisions until about a half an hour into their hour practice.*

*He wore an obvious look of disapproval. "I think that last note could be an octave higher. You just need to be sure to breathe from your diaphragm and not from your chest. Breathing from your chest will not allow you the air you need to hit the high note." He explained."*

*Kyla respected Dr. Winston's opinion and she completely agreed with his assessment. She made a few attempts to hit the almost impossible note with no success.*

*"Here, let me show you." Dr. Winston offered.*

*Kyla watched as he pushed his stool away from the piano. His six-foot-five-inch frame towered over her as he approached her from behind.*

*"Okay, here we go."*

*Her heart began to palpitate when he reached his arms around her and place his large hands on her abdomen, with his semi-erect penis pressing against the middle of her back.*

*"Now, inhale." He coached.*

*Kyla felt as if she would hyperventilate. But, she thought about who this was. Dr. Winston was her favorite teacher. Surely, he wouldn't do anything inappropriate, right? She calmed herself and inhaled as instructed.*

*"Now exhale."*

*She complied.*

*"See how my fingers separate and come back together? That's how you know you're breathing properly. Panting will help you to exercise that muscle. Try it."*

*He placed his hands on her stomach again, and she began to pant.*

*"Mmmm." Dr. Winston moaned deeply.*

*Kyla thought it may have been her imagination, until she felt his partial erection grow and his hands slowly travel upward to her breast.*

*Her heart started to pound, and her initial fears were confirmed. It was after school hours and she was afraid to make a spectacle for fear of being forcefully assaulted. So, she calmed herself and thought of her next move.*

*"I think I've got it, Dr. Winston. Like this, right?"*

*She stepped away from the inappropriate teacher and placed her hands on her own stomach and began to pant.*

*"Y-yes. That's right." He nervously replied.*

*Kyla took a step backward, picking up her belongings on her way to the door.*

*"Okay. Well, I'll work on what you taught me today."*

*Without dismissal or permission, Kyla voluntarily ended the rehearsal thirty minutes early and walked out the door. She swiftly headed to the nearest exit, watching her back all the way. She couldn't believe her favorite teacher had just sexually violated her. Tears streamed down her face at the reality of it all.*

*Once outside, she stopped momentarily to catch her breath and wipe her tears. She looked around the mostly empty high-school campus, and it felt surreal. Who does she tell? What will she say?*

*The sound of a student exiting the door behind her, startled Kyla and caused her to take off running.*

She didn't stop until she was blocks away from the school. Her ride home was supposed to be the school's activity bus. But she would rather walk home in the cold than stay on campus for another minute, let alone another hour. She chose instead to take the three-mile walk.

During her walk, her mind constantly replayed the image of Dr. Winston breaking her trust and violating her innocence. Even at age sixteen, she hadn't even experimented with a boy, God forbid a grown man. She wanted so badly to run into her father's arms and cry unrelentingly. But, she couldn't; she wouldn't. She wasn't sure if she trusted him either.

Since the day she saw her father with another woman, their relationship had been distant, almost non-existent. For almost a year Kyla had avoided her father and was still very angry with him. And then, when she would see how his continued infidelity affected her mother, she became livid all over again. Sometimes she even felt she hated him.

After an hour and fifteen-minute walk, Kyla finally made it home. But she hesitated to go inside and stood on the porch holding her school books to her chest. As much as she felt that Dr. Winston needed to be exposed, she also knew it would mean exposing herself as well. How would her classmates look at her? What if he denies everything and it's her word against his? She felt a knot in her stomach and felt like she would throw up, causing her to make her way into the house.

With one hand over her mouth and the other hand holding her stomach, Kyla made her way to the downstairs bathroom to purge her emotions, as well as, her stomach. She stood in the mirror after wiping her face and started to feel sick to her stomach again.

"What did I do wrong?" She cried, before throwing up again.

Feelings of guilt flooded her emotions and she couldn't overcome the thought that somehow, maybe she made Dr. Winston think that his advances were okay. Did she appear too eager to sing for him? Did she ask for this somehow? She began to replay prior interactions with her vocal coach in her mind, analyzing each memory for any evidence of fault of her own.

There was about a half an hour before anyone would be home, and she would have to face the reality of transparency or pretend the day never happened. The thought of either caused her severe anxiety. Kyla made a mad dash for the dining room where she remembered seeing her mother take her sorrows out on a bottle of tequila.

"Where is it?"

Kyla frantically searched through the etagere for Shilynne's stash where she found a small bag halfway filled with tiny airplane bottles of tequila. She hurriedly stuffed three bottles into her pocket before moving to the ashtray to salvage the longest cigarette butts. Immediately, she retreated to the back yard. Leaning against the rearmost part of the house, she lit the longest cigarette butt she could find.

After a bout of uncontrollable coughing, the momentary high only made her want to explore what the tequila had to offer. She took out a shot and downed it in a single swallow. She could tell that the burn from the cigarette made the shot go down easier that it would have otherwise. As she rested against the *house and allowed the faux sense of relaxation to take over her body, the event of a couple of hours before seemed to have lost its emotional momentum. She made her way to her room and journaled her tipsy account of the evening.*

That night is a blur to Kyla. Reading the entry jogs her memory some, but she has numbed her pain with tequila for so many years, she hasn't realized the effect this has had on her until now. Refusing to reveal her assault to anyone, not even friends, has only caused the incident to fester into a life of unhealthy and dishonest relationships with men; including her father and brother. Not to mention, she never sang for anyone again. And she feels now that subconsciously she was emotionally destroyed by the fact that the only person to inquire about her singing was her Aunt Ce Ce. Her mother had become too drunk and unattached to notice a difference, and her dad was too ashamed to interact with her.

Kyla sheds a tear at the thought of Caleb, Theo and Shilynne. Out of habit, she pours another shot and starts to pull a cigarette from the pack.

"I wonder how many other girls there were." She said aloud, thinking of other potential victims.

She wonders how many girls after her had to endure Dr. Winston's perversion. As far as she knows he is still teaching music at her high school to this day. And then she realizes that the cause and effect go much further that her relationships. She has also condemned herself to death with the excessive use of cigarettes and alcohol. She pushes the shot away and the cigarette back into the pack. Not even sure if she's prepared for the change she intends to make, or even if it matters, Kyla jots another personal note in her journal.

Kyla,

Smoking and drinking help you to cope about as much as it makes you an adult. You do not need to bury your problems in the bottom of a *bottle. You have parents that love you regardless to what they are going through.*

*And NEVER let anyone stifle your voice.*

*Sing songbird, sing!*

After reading and making notes to herself in several more of her old journals, Kyla goes to the bathroom to look in the mirror. As she looks at herself, she realizes that she has been afraid to become the person she is supposed to be. She has allowed disfunction, distrust, and insecurity to mold her into a person that she doesn't even care for. Being complacent with the company surrounding her made it certain that she would eventually conform, which she has. Now, she wonders if it's too late to change.

Tears cover her face and they seem to dissipate all of the disappointment, self-pity, shame, and pride that has left her spiritually and emotionally stagnant for so long. She washes her face, and she prays and cries out to God in desperation. She knows that the possibility of anything she has done tonight making any difference, is impossible.

But the night has offered her so much more. More than what most get to experience before crossing over; self-reflection. Above all else, her journals give her the opportunity to evaluate her life and the choices that has gotten her to this place. She spends hours talking to God like he is right in front of her, until she finally falls off to sleep in the middle of the living room floor, surrounded by a pile of journals.

# Chapter Twenty-Three

## "So, It Shall Be"

Birds chirping so loudly they sound like they are in the room, startle Kyla awake. And the sun is shining so brightly she can hardly focus her eyes, and she can't ever remember the sun shining that brightly into her bedroom window before. Not to mention, she can't remember how she managed to get back to her bedroom from her evening of self-reflection and falling asleep on the living room floor.

"Why am I laying at the foot of the bed?" She asks herself, noticing the sun shining from the opposite side of the room than usual.

She rubs the film from her eyes and stretches as she sits up in bed to discover she is not laying at the foot of the bed at all. Kyla pulls the covers to her chest and prays her Cancer hasn't spread further into her brain. The bedroom is foreign, and she only recognizes some of the items in the elegant but alien bedroom. The décor of the room is mostly gold and white, and the furniture seems larger than life.

"Did I die in my sleep?" She continues to question her reality. "Maybe I'm dreaming."

Kyla pinches her forearm as hard as she can.

"Ow! Definitely not dreaming." She says, rubbing her arm.

Now afraid of what else she may find to be different than what she remembers, Kyla slowly eases out of bed. She walks around the room admiring and rubbing her fingers across the furniture and draperies. Suddenly, the doorknob begins to twist and the door bursts open.

"Donovan!" Kyla screams.

She rushes to the bed and pulls the blanket over her half naked body.

"What are y. . . ?"

"Good. You're awake. Hurry up and get dressed." He points toward the closet. "Everyone is coming here to ride in the limo." Donovan says cutting her off and then he immediately exits the room before she can utter another syllable.

"Everyone?" She is even further confused.

She rushes to the window to see a limousine already parking in the circular driveway of the huge house.

"Where am I?"

Kyla searches through the designer bag on the dresser and retrieves a cell phone. She frantically dials Celeste's phone number. Pacing an imaginary hole in the floor, she nervously waits as the phone continues to ring. Finally, she answers.

"Hello sweetheart!" Celeste sounds cheerful.

"Auntie! Where are you?"

"I'm on my way to ride with you in the limo. Is everything alright?"

Kyla thinks back to her missing scar and her interaction with Arron and his family at the store after a night of making memos in her journals.

"Yes Auntie. Everything is fine. I'll see you when you get here." She decides not to panic just yet.

Kyla hangs up the phone and begins to dress for Caleb's funeral. Being on unfamiliar territory, she thought it would be difficult, but it's just the opposite. She seems to know instinctively where everything is. When she makes her way into the attached bathroom to shower, amazement is the best way to describe how she feels. The bathroom is everything she could have ever wished for; a rainforest shower, a television, and the deepest jacuzzi tub she has ever seen in a house. The his and her vanity makes her wonder who the all too familiar house actually belongs to. She decides she will take full advantage of the shower and gets dressed for the funeral.

Forty-five minutes later, Kyla emerges from the bedroom into a huge hallway covered with green and gold Victorian carpeting and large handcrafted wooden doorways lined up on each side. She wears black from head to toe with only a gold belt and clutch to break up the monotony. As she slowly makes her way down the hallway, she takes notice of every painting, statue, drapery, and lighting. The house resembles something from Luxury Homes Magazine, and she is eager to find Donovan, so she can ask all the unanswered questions that has plagued her since awakening in this beautiful but strange place.

"Kay Kay!" Kyla is relieved to hear Celeste's voice coming from downstairs.

"I'm up here!" Kyla calls down to her.

Kyla immediately embraces her aunt, holding in all the emotion radiating through her.

"I'm so happy to see you Auntie."

"I'm always happy to see you, Mon Coeur." Celeste takes a step back and looks at Kyla's attire. "What are you wearing sweetheart? Don't you think you should wear something with a little more color?"

"I thought black would be appropriate." Kyla is confused. "Auntie, where are we? Whose house is this?"

Celeste chuckles and places her hand on Kyla's forehead. "Are you feeling alright, child?"

"To be honest, I'm not sure."

Just then, Donovan appears on the top step, seemingly out of nowhere.

"Okay, ladies it's almost time to head out!" He announces, before looking at Kyla. "Are you wearing that?"

Kyla parts her lips but is interrupted as Donovan continues.

"I guess it doesn't matter. You're beautiful wearing anything."

She blushes, but before she can say thank you Donovan disappears downs the stairs.

"Well, let's get to it." Celeste says, offering Kyla her arm.

The two lock arms and head down the steps. Celeste converses with Kyla, but she can't stop looking at the rest of the house as it is revealed with every descending step. The wide-open floor plan shows off a room gorgeously furnished and decorated in greenery.

"Beautiful." Kyla whispers under her breath.

Despite her destination of mourning, this room gives her a sense of peace that she hasn't had since she was a child and long before life became so complicated. But just as quickly as the peace comes, it leaves.

"Hi Kyla!" Skye's chipper voice radiates through the room.

Again, her invasion of space is taken by surprise as she embraces Kyla, pulling her toward her small baby bump.

"Oh, um Skye, right?" Kyla asks.

Celeste and Skye look curiously at one another before they embrace.

"Hi Aunt Ce Ce." Skye says.

Figuring they know one another from church, Kyla refrains from questioning why Skye would address Celeste in such a manner. As far as she knows, she and Caleb were the only people that address her as "aunt" anything, and she's is not quite sure how she feels about it. The sting of jealousy causes Kyla to give Skye a dirty look without even noticing.

Heaven bursts through the front door and announces her own presence.

"Everyone can relax now! I'm here!"

She makes her way around the room to greet all three women.

"Where's my big head brother?" Heaven asks Kyla.

"How should I know? He's somewhere around this mammoth of a house. "

"I'm in here!" Donovan yells from the kitchen.

Heaven retreats to the kitchen and instant laughter ensures between the twin siblings.

An uncomfortable silence takes place among Kyla, Skye, and Celeste as they stand in the living room.

"Sweetheart, why don't you get off those feet and have a seat." Celeste tells Skye.

She scoffs at Kyla as if she has done something wrong.

"Excuse us Skye." Celeste says.

She grabs Kyla firmly by the elbow and all but drags her into the adjoining room, which Kyla notices is equally as elegant. She assumes it is a family room because of the pictures that appear to be family oriented displayed throughout the room.

"Ow!" Kyla winces at the pain in her elbow. "What!?"

"Why are you being so rude?" Celeste scolds her.

Kyla realizes that things a certainly different than when she fell asleep the night before, but since she is unaware of how much, she wants to refrain from seeming delusional until she can get some real clarity.

"I'm not trying to Auntie. I just feel a little off, that's all." Kyla rubs her temples. "I should probably sit down too."

196

But before she has the chance to take a seat, Donovan calls her into the kitchen. She gives Celeste a confused glance.

"Well, go see what the man wants!" Celeste prompts her as she mumbles something in creole to herself.

Kyla starts toward the kitchen and gives a side eye to Skye to see her reaction, but all she sees is her checking her watch and looking out of the window as if waiting for someone to arrive. She continues into the kitchen where Heaven and Donovan lean against the counter standing side by side. Donovan's face lights up when Kyla enters the room, much like when they were teens. Heaven recognizes that look and decides to go into the living room, leaving the two alone.

"So, how are you feeling? You ready for today?" He asks.

"As ready as I'm going to be." Kyla says somberly.

Kyla continues further into the huge kitchen and looks around like a tourist. Suddenly, she feels Donovan's hands around her waist. Her first thought is

197

to resist, but she allows him to turn her body so that they are facing one another. She feels secure as he moves in closer, towering over her, but sheltering her at the same time. She is so caught up in the moment she doesn't even realize that her eyes are closed, until she feels Donovan's gentle kiss on her lips and his sensuous embrace.

"What are you doing?" Kyla asks, jumping out of Donovan's arms and stepping a few feet away. "What about Skye?"

"Skye?" Donovan appears baffled.

"I mean, I know I acted weird and jealous when I saw you two at church the other day, but this is not right. I just can't!" Kyla is appalled by his actions. "And whose house is this any way!?" She yells out of frustration from being disconcerted.

Donovan slowly approaches Kyla and pulls out a chair for her to sit.

"Babe, I know you've got to be nervous about singing at The Fox Theatre for the first time, but are you sure you're alright?"

"Singing? What are you talking about?" Kyla feels like she is spinning out of control.

But before Donovan can part his lips to respond, the kitchen door swings open.

"Let's get this show on the road, Superstar!"

Kyla can't believe her eyes. She is frozen in the chair and she can't move. Her mouth is hanging open, but no air is going in or coming out. She becomes light-headed and dizzy, and almost falls out of her seat. Donovan rushes to her side to catch her and her tear-filled eyes meet his.

"Baby, what's the matter?" His face is etched with sheer concern. "You look like you've seen a ghost."

She looks again toward the doorway to see Skye hand-in-hand with Caleb.

"Sis, I know you're not performing in that. You look like you're headed to a funeral."

Kyla runs to Caleb and jumps into his arms. Tears stream down her face as she plants countless kisses on his.

199

"I love you so much! Do you know that?" Kyla cries.

"Um, I love you too?" Caleb is perplexed by her sudden display of affection.

"Well, isn't this beautiful?"

Kyla's recognition of the loving female voice coming from behind Caleb, causes her to break down to her knees. Just then, Shilynne and Theo walk into the kitchen together to see Kyla on her knees face down on the floor, bawling uncontrollably.

The kitchen is now filled with family concerned about what is happening. Kyla sits up and attempts to open her eyes. Suddenly, flashes of light resembling a lightening storm inside her head begin to reveal flashes from her past. Again, memories unexperienced start to haunt her recollection as her reality is pushed to the background of her psyche. She grabs her own head as an attempt to stop the flashes but is unsuccessful.

Her remembrance echoes her current reality. She now sees flashes of her and Caleb in a loving sibling relationship, then her father's presence where he had been absent before, including conversations

200

about his cheating and her experience with Dr. Winston, and then flashes of Dr. Winston in handcuffs. Also, her mother alive and her parents together and happy. She sees images of her performing in front of thousands with Heaven by her side. But most profound is the memory of her and Donovan's wedding. Before she can emotionally expound on what has been unleashed, the flashes stop just as suddenly as they had come.

Unbeknownst to Kyla, Donovan has picked her up and carried her to a couch in the family room. The concerned family surrounds her as she opens her eyes. Her emotions have now caught up with her realized reality, and Donovan is the first person she sees. She grabs his hand and pulls him as close as she can.

"Baby are you alright?" He asks.

"I'm more than alright. I love you! I've been in love with you since I was fourteen years old."

She pulls his face to hers and kisses him more passionately than she can ever recall kissing anyone before, as a joyful tear trickles from the corner of her eye and down her cheek.

Kyla jumps up from the couch and rushes to her mom and dad. "I'm so happy to see you both!" She squeezes them both as tightly as she can, and exchanges kisses back and forth between them.

During her embrace, she notices the pictures on the wall behind her parents and recognizes the combination chest in the corner. She hurriedly rushes over to the portraits to see the immortalized images of her family as she sees them today. Her family watches on with confused curiosity as she hastily dials the combination into the chest. She pulls out the first journal, which happens to be the sunflower journal that Donovan gave her for her fourteenth birthday. She frantically searches through the pages looking for the note she left herself years ago. She pauses when she notices the journal's contents are different from before. It is filled with time she shared with Donovan and moments spent with Heaven and Micah.

Kyla flips to the beginning of the book and finally finds what she is looking for. But, even that entry is not the same. In fact, as she looks closer at the page she can see that the note she left herself in the corner has been erased, and the events of that day are totally different. She then looks at the clock on the wall and quickly closes the chest.

"I'll be right back!"

She runs out of the door, grabbing her keys on the way.

"Kyla, you have to be at sound check in an hour!" Donovan yells as she pulls out of the circular driveway.

As much as the flashbacks show her, there are still some things that are unclear. Like, where is Jameca, and what is her health status? Kyla looks at herself in the rearview mirror and her eyes look clearer and brighter than ever before. Then she realizes she hasn't had or wanted a cigarette or a drink. But why? Did prayer and one night of writing notes to herself in journals cause her entire life to change? And then, she can hear the voices of Celeste, Heaven, and the preacher at the church speak about unmovable faith and Valerie from group talk about her contribution to

203

history. One thing that Kyla remembers for sure about the night before is how she completely surrendered to God. She was content with whatever His outcome was for her life and she trusted Him regardless to what that outcome was, and she still does.

She can honestly attest that she has never felt this way before. And never before would she have placed this kind of trust in an entity she can't see. But what she realizes is that she has truly evolved. She is a speaking spirit that inhabits a natural body created by God. The reflection over her life the night before, makes her realize how valuable she is to not only her own life, but to the life of those around her. She now realizes that God has created her as a vessel, and every time she neglects the post that God has placed her, a soul is neglected and is therefore placed in jeopardy, just as her mother, father, and brother had been. So, operating in her full potential is important. Now she realizes how far the influence of one person can reach when she thinks about her life without Donovan and her mother, but most important, without faith in her Lord and Savior.

Ready to accept whatever her current fate has to offer, she pulls in to the parking lot of the medical building and says a short prayer before entering. Finally, she walks into the doctors' office lobby.

"Hi Linda. Is Dr. Okai available for a few minutes?"

Linda look at the schedule on her computer. "It looks like Dr. Okai is with a patient. Who should I tell her would like to see her?"

"Kyla LaRue?" Kyla answers as if to remind Linda of who she is.

The receptionist searches the patient log. "Are you a new patient?" She seems confused.

"No. I've been coming here for almost a year."

"Okay, let me try something else."

Linda pulls up Kyla's name in a general search and sees that her name has changed.

"Oh, here you are, Kyla King. You are Dr. Assad's patient. And according to this he has been trying to reach you with your test results."

"What test?" Kyla inquires.

"Let me see if he's available to speak with you."

The receptionist makes a call to confirm the doctor's availability.

"He is available and will see you now. Right this way." Linda escorts her into the doctor's office.

Kyla enters the room to see a man that only looks slightly familiar sitting behind a large wooden desk.

"Dr. Assad?" Kyla sounds unsure.

"Yes Mrs. King. Your husband isn't joining you today?"

"No sir. I really just wanted to check on my Cancer progression."

"Cancer?" The doctor frantically flips through Kyla's medical records.

"Yes. Linda said you wanted to see me about my test results."

"Oh!" The doctor is obviously relieved.

"Ma'am, your results have nothing to do with Cancer, I assure you. But I thought you both would be here. Anyway, here you go." He hands her a sealed envelope.

"What's this?"

"It's the results to your hCG blood test, for pregnancy."

Kyla immediately rips open the envelope to see that the test is positive.

"So, you mean I don't have Cancer?" She is adamant about a reply to that question specifically.

"Mrs. King, you are a perfectly healthy mother-to-be." He assures her.

Tears stream down her cheeks without any effort on her part, and she rubs her belly.

"Thank you doctor." Kyla jumps up to hug the unsuspecting doctor. "Thank you, God!"

Dr. Assad looks on uncomfortably as Kyla drops to her knees and continues to cry and thank God.

"Are you alright Mrs. King?" The doctor asks as he helps her to her feet.

"I am wonderful doctor! Better than I've been in a long time!" She smiles.

She exits the building and stops to take time out to feel the sun on her face. With her eyes closed and her head tilted toward the sky, Kyla allows the sun to wash over her. The warmth of the sun begins to cool and when she opens her eyes the sky darkens as if it were filled with dark grey storm clouds, but there are none.

The wind starts to blow so furiously Kyla feels she will be lifted off her feet. Just then, the atmosphere around her fades and she is sucked into a vortex of the past. As she is uncontrollably plunged through space and time, she can see her life in reverse as it flashes before her. Unafraid, she allows the chronological force to take control. In moments, she feels the sensation of falling, as she plummets downward and lands with tremendous impact.

When Kyla opens her eyes again, she is lying faceup in her childhood bed, and the calendar reads March 22nd with "Kyla's 14th birthday" written in her own handwriting. She rolls over and rapidly sits up in bed. The clock on the nightstand reads 5:45 am, and the house is completely silent. She rubs her hands across the comforter on her bed to be sure this is real. Looking around the room, she is able to identify every individual item as her own. She walks over to the mirror to see her fourteen-year-old self, staring back at her.

"Why am I back here?" She asks as she touches her own face.

She looks around the room and it is just as she remembers. The pink walls, the off-white wooden furniture, the floral curtains and comforter, along with the familiar smell of fresh linen in the air. But as comfortable as she is in this space, she is even more confused. And then she remembers this day and how it has symbolically been the first day of the rest of her life. After this day, she began to relinquish the Kyla she is supposed to become, to the Kyla most accepted. Now she wonders if she has been given a second chance to become the best version of herself.

209

She looks again at herself in the mirror. "So, it shall be. Here's to your second chance to make a first impression."

Right on cue, Caleb bursts through the door with a pillow in hand ready to attack Kyla with her first birthday blow. But, she isn't in bed. He looks confused momentarily and turns to leave the room. Suddenly, Kyla jumps from behind the door and wraps both arms around Caleb.

"Gotcha!"

She starts showering him with tiny kisses all over his face.

"Ew! Stop it!" Caleb screams.

"Nope. It's my birthday and I want to give you kisses." She retorts.

Caleb stops struggling and reluctantly takes the kisses.

"This is gross, you know."

"I know, but I love you little brother and, I need you to know that no matter how much we argue I love you more than anything in this world, and I'm sorry for all the mean things I've said and done to you. I'm fourteen now. It's time for me to grow up and be a better example for you."

Caleb gives Kyla a peculiar stare. "Are you okay?"

"I'm better than okay." She smiles at him.

"Well, I love you too." He quickly says before readily exiting her room.

Kyla looks over at her already pressed birthday outfit and decides to wear something different. She searches her closet and finds her favorite outfit; a white cotton T-shirt dress with sunflowers all over it. She quickly dresses and makes her way downstairs to the kitchen. On her way down the steps, she immediately remembers her fourteenth birthday breakfast. She can already smell pancakes and a plethora of breakfast meats, and she can hear her mother's and Caleb's voice. She is pleasantly surprised when she enters to find her father sitting at the table across from her mother's famous birthday cakes: Pancakes, topped with whipped cream, strawberries, and chocolate syrup; Kyla's favorite.

"Happy birthday, beautiful!" Shilynne belts.

"Happy birthday, baby girl!" Theo says looking up from his morning paper.

"Thank you!"

"You look really pretty today, birthday girl!" Celeste says.

"Thanks Mom." Kyla smiles.

"She looks alright." Caleb says dryly.

"Well thank you, brat." Kyla laughs.

The family enjoys breakfast together and Kyla cherishes every second. She looks around the table and finds if difficult to take her eyes off of her family. Seeing her mother's face and hearing her voice warms her soul. And her father's presence makes her feel like the special little girl she was always meant to feel like.

"I just want to say, I love you guys." Kyla tells her family.

"We love you too, baby girl." Theo says.

Kyla finishes her birthday breakfast and proceeds to meet her friends. As she approaches the corner where she meets Jameca and her crew every morning, she can see four mylar balloons, one held by each girl, bouncing in her direction. All four girls are in matching dresses in different colors.

"Happy birthday, beeeach!" Jameca screams from yards away.

All four girls excitedly run in Kyla's direction and bombard her with hugs and balloons.

"Aw, thank yawl!"

"Girl, you know birthdays are special, especially if you're one of my girls!" Jameca exclaims. "Where's your dress?" Jameca asks, noticing that Kyla is not wearing their planned attire.

"Oh, I decided since it's my birthday, I wanted to be different. So, I picked out something else."

Jameca gives a look of disapproval at the thought of Kyla having an individual notion but decides against making an issue of it, but only because it's Kyla's birthday.

The five fashionable and fit, fabulous teenage girls make their way to the bus stop. Kyla, with four balloons in tow, feels like the most important person in the world. But she can't wait to get to school so that she can see Donovan.

While on the bus, the group of girls indulge in mindless chatter, oblivious to the boys around them gawking as if sharing a bus ride with celebrities. Only Kyla looks around the bus and individually takes notice of each person, before she's interrupted by her needy companion.

"So, Ky, what did your dad say about letting you have a birthday / spring break party?" Jameca asks.

"I'm not really interested in a birthday / spring break party. I just want to hang out and have fun. Oh, and I think I'm cancelling my date with Travis. I don't really want to go to the dance with him."

"But Kyla! What about Derek? We were supposed to be going with them together. He only asked me because Travis wants to go to the dance with you, remember?"

"Jameca, you are the most popular girl in school. I'm sure you won't have any issues keeping your date with Derek. Besides, I've decided I'm not going to settle because someone else wants me to. I don't like Travis, and I'm not going to pretend to like him just to please you. I'm sorry."

"You suck!" Jameca expresses as the bus approaches the school.

Even with all of the excitement surrounding her birthday, the only thing Kyla can think about is Donovan. She has tiptoed around her feelings for him and her desire to spend quality time with him, but now all bets are off. She doesn't care what anyone thinks or what anyone knows.

"Hey, I'll catch up with you all later." Kyla announces.

"Where you finna go?" Jameca inquires.

"Well, if you must know, I'm going to meet Donovan at his locker." She says with her head held high.

"You mean, Inch High Private Eye?" Jameca laughs with her minions.

"No, I mean Donovan King, not inch-high or shorty or lil bit! His name is Donovan and he doesn't deserve to be called names because YOU don't approve of his height or think he's popular enough." Kyla rolls her eyes.

"Aw snap! You're serous? You're taking up for him and everything! So, you like Inch Hi. . . I'm sorry, I mean Donovan?"

"Yes, I do." Kyla's stare is intense. "In fact, what I have come to realize is that it's you that I don't like very much. You're mean, rude, disrespectful, arrogant, and needy. And then, on top of all of that, you're insecure. I feel sorry for you." She turns and looks at the other three girls in the group. "If you all had any backbone, you would tell her how you really feel too!"

Jameca is visibly livid and decides to try Kyla on for size. She walks up to Kyla toe-to-toe, eye-to-eye.

"Little girl, no one would even know who you were if it wasn't for me. I made you!" Jameca spit the words out like venom.

As if it were possible for the two to get any closer, Kyla lets go of her balloons, allowing them to hit the ceiling as she takes a step closer to Jameca causing her to stumble slightly backward into the lockers.

"God made me." Kyla gives her a penetrating glare before walking away with finality.

The students in the hallway look around to see if anyone knows what could have transpired so quickly as Jameca attempts to recover from her embarrassment.

"Fuck you, Bitch! We don't need you anyway!"

Kyla hurriedly makes a beeline for Donovan's locker. Just as she hoped, there he stands, gathering his books for his next two classes. She slowly makes her way next to his locker and stands on the other side of his open locker door.

"Boo!" Kyla startles Donovan as he closes the door.

Clearly surprised, he drops his English book along with a thin gift-wrapped package. Kyla is flattered that she makes him so nervous. They both bend down to pick up his belongings and Donovan notices the print of her dress and smiles. They reach for the English book at the same time and their fingers lightly touch, but the lingering eye contact seems to last forever, until Donovan abruptly ends the moment and quickly moves his hand from the book and onto the package.

"Um, this is for you. Happy Birthday."

"Thank you." She smiles without pulling her eyes away from his.

"Aren't you going open it?"

"Oh, yes! I'm sure whatever it is, I'll love it."

She excitedly rushes to open the package as if she is oblivious to its contents, to reveal the pastel colored journal with sunflowers on the cover, that reads

'I hope your day shines as bright as you do'. She holds the journal against her dress.

"I guess this was the perfect gift, huh?" Kyla says. "I love it, thank you again."

"I remembered you told the class sunflowers were your favorite flower."

"Well, something tells me that I will make very good use of this." She smiles. "Can I ask you something?"

He closes his locker and gives her his undivided attention.

"Sure."

"Will you go to the spring dance with me?" She is confident but still I bit nervous.

"Is this a joke between you and your friends or something?" Donovan immediately becomes defensive. "I hear it when they say stuff about me, but I didn't think you would stoop this low."

"What? No! I can't be that person anymore. I'm not that person. And we kind of fell out this morning."

"So, you really want to go to the dance with me?" Donovan is perplexed.

"More than anything." She says with a sincere smile.

"I'd be honored to go with you."

Only Kyla knows that this will be the first of many, as she leans in and gives Donovan their first and most innocent kiss. They smile at one another and Kyla offers her hand, and they walk hand-in-hand to class together, for the first time.

*The End*

*"Remember always that your actions in life may be the very action that causes the evolution or the demise of those connected to you. Be aware of the post God has placed you, and don't abandon it!"* ~ *Laveau White*

Made in the USA
Monee, IL
04 December 2021